CUTTER'S WAKE

CUTTER'S WAKE

•

Lynn M. Turner

AVALON BOOKS
NEW YORK

To my brother,
Jamie MacKenzie

Chapter One

Susan Stead figured she'd outstayed her welcome at the Seal Harbor Restaurant and Social Club. She couldn't drink another cup of coffee anyway; her whole body felt twitchy with caffeine. Outside, the light spilling from the windows created broad bars of pale gray lines across the dark parking lot. She breathed in the salty air and, slowly turning, contemplated the shadowy forms of saltbox houses and the flat, unadorned facade of the restaurant. A faint twang of a country-and-western song drifted from a nearby fish-packing plant, and the trees across the street rustled in the breeze.

She briskly rubbed her chilled arms. Halifax and her own condo were a forty-minute drive away, but she wasn't ready to go home just yet. There was one last thing she wanted to do. She slid into her car's driver's seat, turned the key, and flipped on the headlights.

As the car purred along she put down the window and leaned an elbow outside. A mist rolled in from the ocean

1

and lay in the dips of the narrow road, forming pools of eerie murkiness, but the air on the high ground remained clear, almost crisp.

She slowed the car to crawl over the rough drive at the entrance to the beach. The bouncing beam from her headlights illuminated the empty first parking area. Susan didn't want her car to be visible so she bumped along and stopped where she was hidden behind a mound of sand and gravel. When the car finished creaking and settling, the sound of waves filled her ears. After a moment she climbed out and closed the door softly behind her. The air was pungent with the tangy smell of gin berries and wet peat.

It felt eerie, being on the beach alone, in the dark. She'd been here hundreds of times, usually with a crowd, but on this night she needed to be by herself.

She hugged her arms and listened intently. Amy, the little girl she had befriended on the beach, lived nearby. Her house wasn't visible; a round hill fell between it and this end of the beach. Still, knowing that someone lived within walking distance bolstered Susan's courage. She fetched some old sneakers from the trunk and changed into them.

The moonlight made walking across the rock-strewn path possible, but where boulders cast their shadows the ground yawned pitch black. Susan emerged onto the beach and caught her breath—startled at the whiteness of the moon-bathed sand. It was painfully beautiful: the blue silver of the water, the puffy white mist billowing softly over its surface, and the phosphorescence sparkling in the foam.

Susan decided that this was exactly what she needed. The beach, the ocean, had always restored her in the past. She had been going through a difficult time at work lately because she could no longer dredge up any enthusiasm for selling office equipment. In fact, she didn't feel at home anywhere these days. Even her condo, which had seemed plush and beautiful a year before, now felt alien. She needed to make a change, she knew, but to what? She would just sit here on her favorite spot on earth and make some decisions about her life.

Far offshore the Seal Harbor Lighthouse stabbed its clear white line through the mist across the water. Ten seconds later the beam made its way around again. The gentle swells of the ocean touched first to her left so that the hiss of them breaking over the sand traveled from one side to the other. Slow and rhythmic, over and over again. Susan started back up the incline to find drier sand. She lowered her lanky body onto the sand, pulled her knees up to her chest, and thought.

The sound of voices intermingled with the wash of the surf so stealthily that she first thought she imagined them. People were approaching. Susan, both apprehensive and loath to break the spell of the night, eased into the black shadow of a rock. There she waited, hoping that the intruders would go away.

They came closer.

Frightening visions scraped across her mind: taunting drunks throwing bottles, her car being ransacked, eyes finding her. Ignoring the slime and mud oozing under her fingers, Susan squeezed deeper into the darkness between the boulders. She stiffened at the unexpected wail of a child and, for an instant, felt relief—they were family people, not violent drunks. But, listening to the pitiful cries, she soon felt concern. That child was in pain. Should she expose herself to offer assistance?

Now, over the sound of the surf and wailing of the child, she made out crunching footsteps. A blue shadow moved over the sand.

"I want my mummy!" The child shrieked. "Mummy!"

Susan poked her head around the edge of her rock. Two men, one of them clutching a struggling little girl, hurried along the beach. The child thrashed back and forth, kicking and scratching.

"Shut her up, will ya, Perry," the man on the left growled.

Susan got a good look at Perry, the one holding the girl. He had fair hair, blond or gray, that receded into two bald points on his scalp but hung in limp waves a few inches down his back, and he wore a T-shirt over baggy-kneed pants. He adjusted the child's weight and dropped her roughly to the sand. Appalled, Susan started to stand.

The second man held the tiny form down by the shoulders. "Give me the scarf," he barked.

Susan's mouth hung open. She was struck dumb as the two men wound a rag across the child's whimpering mouth. They were gagging a tiny little girl!

Susan was an athletic woman, tall and fit. Even so, if she'd given her actions any thought, she would have hesitated. Instead instinct kicked in and she scrambled toward the men. "What are you doing? What's going on?"

One of the men recoiled in surprise, then, with his eyes locked on hers, climbed warily to his feet. As he advanced the angular features on the left side of his face were sharpened by the moonlight but the right side was hidden in black shadow. His dark hair, cut short over his ears, fell forward in an oily curl between his eyes. He had the cuffs of his denim jacket rolled to just below the elbow and a bulky chain was tight against his wrist.

Susan jerked to a stop at the expression in his eyes— wild, angry, terrifying. Then, behind him, she caught a glimpse of a tiny leg and a fluorescent-orange shoelace. Anger overcame her fear. "Do you want to tell me what is going on here?"

"Mind your own business," he said thickly.

The little girl made a mad dash for freedom but Perry

caught her easily in mid-flight. She shrieked and bit savagely. Time seemed to stand still as her little sneakers swung in midair. Susan gasped.

"Amy?" she asked. "Is that you, Amy?"

Her mind scrambled for any possible reason to account for their behavior. Amy lived nearby, in the big mansion overlooking the beach. Maybe these were her uncles, or something? After all, although Susan had played with Amy on the beach many times, she didn't know the little girl's family.

"Amy, who are these men? Do you know them?"

Amy squirmed free and rushed into Susan's arms. She was light and tiny, warm and trembling. Susan rocked and cooed to her in a gentle voice, all the while staring stabs of hate at the two ruffians.

The big men advanced cautiously, like hunters circling a wild animal. A hunched Susan clutched the child against her chest; her eyes sized up her attackers and her body shifted for flight. Tiny hairs on her neck and arms stood straight. Through bared teeth she snarled, "Who are you? What are you doing with Amy?" Nothing.

Instantly Susan took to her feet and pounded down the beach. After a dozen steps hands like vise grips grabbed her ankles and she fell headlong.

Chapter Two

Susan landed hard on her right shoulder. Amy flew clear.

"Run!" Susan screamed at the child, and hurled herself on her attacker. *"Run!"*

She clutched at the closest jacket and swung her feet, kicking violently toward the other man. Amy took off.

Perry shoved Susan. Crashing back, she hit her face on the dirt with a jarring crack. It took her a moment to come to her senses, raise her head, and look for Amy. Perry carried Amy across his hip like a sack of flour as she struggled weakly.

"Take her to the dory. I'll get this one."

Perry answered incredulously, "You're bringing *her?*"

"What do *you* think? She saw what we're doing, saw our faces."

Susan froze. What should she do? Run? Abandon Amy and go for help?

"Help!" she screamed, but through the ringing in her ears her voice sounded weak, hoarse. "Help! Help!"

Her head snapped back as the guy grabbed her ponytail. "Shut up or I'll kill you here and now."

Susan believed him even before he thrust the short, nasty barrel of a gun in her face. Shoving her around, he jabbed it between her shoulder blades. She stumbled forward, too frightened to utter a word.

When they caught up to the other guy, he was lifting Amy into a wooden rowboat that was dragged half out of the water. His fist encircled the child's slender arm and she twisted and cringed from the pain.

"You and the kid—back there."

Susan stumbled forward, climbed over the side of the boat, and crawled to the rear. As soon as Amy was released, she clambered over the board seats and climbed beside Susan. Susan's arms encircled her.

A two-way radio appeared in Perry's hand and sputtered to life. The minute he spoke, the crackling stopped. "Okay, come and get us."

The men stood on either side of the dory and worked to shove it into the ocean. They splashed around up to their knees, maneuvered the pointed end outward, and climbed aboard. The dark-haired man took the bow, facing the rower and the captives. His gun gleamed dimly on his lap.

"Think the boat heard us?" Perry asked.

"Yeah, just row."

Susan held Amy tightly and, masking the desperation in her voice, said, "Where are you taking us? Stop and think about this now—you don't have to go through with this."

With his broad back to her, leaning forward and backward with each powerful stroke, Perry grunted. "What a mess." After a few more strokes he lifted the oars to drip over the water. "What do ya say we get rid of them right now, tonight?"

"The kid's got to be alive next week. Besides, it'd be too noisy."

The meaning of the words penetrated Susan's consciousness. *Alive next week.* Only until next week? She looked wildly around her. Could Amy swim? Should she throw her overboard? Capsize the boat?

As though he read her mind, the man in the bow pointed the gun. "I think we can keep them alive for a little while."

Since he faced in the direction of the moon, his evil grin was as clear as if it had been captured in the flash of a camera. She froze.

Over and over again the ocean swells, which grew as they moved farther away from the harbor, lifted the boat in the air and dropped it with a slap. Susan wrapped one arm tightly around Amy's shoulders and clutched firmly onto the boat with her free hand. The sound of the surf receded in the distance.

"Think they heard us?" the rower asked again.

"They're right there."

Susan craned her neck and looked out to sea. A fishing boat running without lights steamed toward them, a squat hull with poles and ropes splaying out the front and high into the air. Soon the throbbing of its engines reverberated in her ears.

She was so frightened that only the need to see Amy safe kept her from making a mad lunge overboard. Breathing in jerky gasps, she tried to calm herself. She looked at Amy, who clung to her with her eyes squeezed closed. The poor little thing. Susan didn't know her well. They'd met a few times on the beach, built a couple of sandcastles together, and Amy even fell asleep on her beach blanket once. That day no one else seemed to notice—no mother or baby-sitter—so Susan herself slathered on the sunblock. Ever since then, she'd felt protective of the lonely child. Now a powerful surge of determination rushed through her.

"Just tell me who you are," she demanded. "Maybe we can work something out. I . . . I've got money. Lots of it."

They ignored her. The sound of the engines changed as the fishing boat glided forward. Susan turned for another look and flinched. The black hull blocked the view. It was coming too fast—it would crush them! She pulled Amy's head to her chest and held on.

But the crew knew what they were doing. The boat glided slowly past with a couple of yards to spare. A minute later, hands reached for them and Susan and Amy were yanked up and on board.

Susan barked her shin crawling over knee-high partitions on the deck. For a moment she floundered, disoriented in the blue light of the moon, and grasped blindly in the direction of Amy's sobs. A hand gripped her elbow and thrust her toward the front of the boat, under an overhanging roof and around behind what looked like a massive coil of electrical wire.

"Wait a minute! Wait a minute!" Her complaints, against the throaty roar of the accelerating diesel engines, barely reached her own ears and were ignored by the man who roughly pressed her to the deck.

She crouched there in the darkness, her arms wrapped tightly around her knees, and trembled uncontrollably. "Where's Amy? Amy?"

Male voices loudly argued. The pitch of the engines changed and Susan leaned sideways with the turn of the boat. Finally a shadow passed in front of her and Amy was dropped into her arms.

The two of them cowered under the overhanging roof. The doors to the interior of the boat were behind them and the open deck hidden from their view because of the five-foot-high coil of rope. Suddenly a light snapped on behind Susan's left shoulder.

Two men, one close behind the other, passed through a small door opening into the hull of the boat and climbed agilely down the ladder. The head and shoulders of a gray-haired man moved back and forth. Occasionally their arguing voices rose above the thumping engines.

How many were on board? Guessing at five, she concentrated on gathering information about her captors: the sound of their voices, the color of their hair.

To the right of the door into the galley, Susan could see another opening into the bridge where a couple of points of light gleamed from the instrument panel. A man moved into view. He looked out the forward windows while his hands worked the levers and dials. Taking note of his jeans and denim shirt, Susan tried to get a look at his features, but he was turned away.

Amy relaxed in her lap and leaned her head on Susan's chest. Susan could feel, but not hear, her whimpering. It was a difficult position. The muscles in her calves tightened.

The man in the bridge turned his head, as though listening, and covered the lower half of his face with his hand. He looked about thirty years old. His belly rounded slightly although the rest of his frame was thin and fit. By the way he moved easily around, Susan guessed the boat belonged to him or that he crewed it regularly.

Suddenly he sprang from his position, took three loping strides, and looked through the opening into the galley. He did not enter, but held onto either side of the doorjamb with his head stuck through.

"Dad! No!" His voice was loud, deep. "No way!"

Susan could not hear the response from the others but it was clearly not the one the man wanted to hear. He yanked his head, as though swearing, and stomped back around the corner to the bridge.

Her leg muscles screamed from the tension, so Susan lifted Amy from her lap and, still hugging her with one arm, placed her on the deck. The voices from the galley stilled. She licked her swollen lips and prepared to go below, to confront these terrifying men.

Suddenly the man from the bridge sprang upon her. She covered her face and shifted to screen Amy's tiny body. He leaned over and clutched her under her armpits. Too shocked to respond, she stumbled to her feet and fell forward. He smelled of sweat and diesel fuel.

He pulled her back under the open sky where she staggered, stumbling over the partitions on the deck. Two seconds later she stood, with her feet braced to balance against the boat's rocking, and stared wild-eyed at the man facing her. A wind created by the speeding boat slapped her hair about her face.

"Stop this boat!" she yelled. "Stop it right now!"

He leaned away to pick something up. It looked brown or orange and when he thrust it into her hands she felt the canvas of a life jacket.

His voice was desperate. "Put it on. Hurry! They're going to kill you. I'm not having anything to do with—" The wind snatched away the rest of the words.

Susan fumbled with the canvas until she had one arm through a hole. "But Amy—?"

He bent, grabbed her about the knees, and tipped her overboard.

It happened very slowly. She saw her feet, knew they were her feet, flying over her head. But there was nothing she could do, nowhere she could hold. She hit the water and went under. Instinct kicked in. With a silent howl, she fought through the inky darkness for the way up, but which was the right direction?

Chapter Three

Susan broke the surface and gasped, only to be slapped hard by a descending wave and shoved back into the nightmare of roiling ocean. Blind instinct sent her thrashing to right herself. Her face cleared the water. Her lungs burned.

Although it was early September, and the ocean was at its warmest, the frigid Atlantic numbed skin and gripped muscles. Tossed up and down on the waves, churning her legs around and around, she fought to overcome the panic.

With a start she remembered the life jacket. It hung precariously from the elbow of her right arm. She held her breath, let the swell wash her under, and concentrated on finding the other armhole. She did nòt bother with the zipper—her fingers were useless anyway—but tied the buckle around her waist in a hard knot.

She churned her arms and legs and looked for the boat. At one point, when the swell had lifted her, she thought she saw its dark hull out toward the ocean. Well, at least no one was shooting at her. Her eyes stung from the salt. A gulp of briny ocean left her coughing and sputtering.

Land was a black silhouette painfully far away. Here and there the lights from a house or cottage beckoned. For a moment she floated up and down trying to decide which spot was closer. Out of the jagged line of the tops of softwood trees stood a particularly tall pine. Aiming herself at it, she kicked off her shoes and started to swim.

Left arm, right arm, left arm, right arm. Visions crowded her mind: the boat, Amy, the evil men. Susan mentally shoved the images aside. The important thing was to get to shore. Then she would call the Royal Canadian Mounted Police. Then she would send the Coast Guard after those scum.

Please God, she prayed, *don't let them hurt Amy.* Susan found a reserve of energy and tapped it. With renewed determination she dug her arms into the water and pulled. For the next hour she swam the awkward strokes caused by the bulky life jacket, head clear of the water. By the time she neared the shore, Susan was swimming in slow motion—pull, kick, pull, kick. Finally her knees scraped the jagged edges of barnacle.

She had made it.

After crawling over bracken and jagged rock, she reached a cottage belonging to an elderly couple who she later learned were Edna and John Wilson. They took her in, soggy life jacket and all, with the calm of trained health care professionals. Even as she sobbed the gist of her story, John Wilson dialed the RCMP.

Danny Shipley, the skipper of the Coast Guard cutter *Seal Harbor,* lived on the edge of the village, a ten-minute drive from the Wilsons' cottage. He was sprawled asleep under a down comforter on his oak four-poster bed. The instant the telephone rang his hand shot out and snatched the receiver.

"Shipley here," he grunted.

His moustache was askew, curled around his upper lip, so he prodded it back into shape with a stiff finger as he listened to the dispatcher explain that he had to find a fishing boat.

"I'm on it."

He hung up, yanked his jeans from the foot of the bed, and pulled them on. As he buttoned his shirt he walked quickly into the living room, across a worn Persian carpet to a side window, and flicked on a small brass lamp. It cast an eerie yellow glow through the glass shade. Across a rocky stretch his parents' house was a squat black silhouette against the moonlit sky. From her window his mother would be able to see the glow of that particular lamp and know that her son was away on another rescue.

She would not worry unduly tonight, he knew, because the sea swelled gently against the shoreline. But when the ocean churned and roiled, when gales crashed against her windows and rain drove in sheets, she worried for her precious son's safety. Those nights Danny always considered leaving the lamp unlit to protect his mother from the anxiety. But he had promised to let her know whenever he had been called on a rescue, and to Danny a promise was a promise.

He had built his little house on an exposed point jutting into Seal Harbor. It was often foggy, always windy, but he reveled in the salt spray and was calmed by the rhythmic crashing of the waves on the steep granite bluff below.

He listened with half an ear to the intensity of the surf as he climbed into his four-wheel-drive truck. Circling the truck around a pile of stove wood, he pointed inland and drove quickly along the graded drive, down the full

length of his promontory, past the wharf and his parents'
house, and onto the main paved road into Seal Harbor.

When Danny climbed out of the truck and loped
toward the station house, Harkey, a gray-haired deckhand who was also responding to the rescue pager,
reached the door before him and fumbled with his keys.

"Cold, eh?" Danny said. He hooked the zipper of his
new jacket and pulled it up snugly around his neck.
Good warmth-to-weight ratio, the advertisement had
said. He believed it. It felt like quality and Danny did
not begrudge spending money on clothing that worked.

Harkey had the door open, stepped in, and snapped
on a brilliant overhead light. "So what's the story?" He
squinted from the glare off the whitewashed walls.

"A kidnapping. Took a woman and a kid out to sea."
Danny reached into a locker and pulled out a brilliant
yellow squall jacket.

Harkey's head snapped up. "Get away with ya!"

"That's what they said." Danny couldn't help smiling
at Harkey's misplaced enthusiasm. The man had lived in
Seal Harbor all his life, worked on the swordfish and
herring boats for close to forty years before joining the
Coast Guard as a deckhand, and still he met each venture
with a boyish raring-to-go attitude.

Harkey whistled through his teeth. "We'll be crawling
with Mounties, eh?"

"Likely." Danny didn't want to linger. They had work
to do. He might be thirty years younger than his deckhand, but he was still the boss. "Go on down and help
John get her going. I'll wait for the details on the fax."

He walked into the inner office. Judging by the bay
windows and ceiling light, it had probably been the living room before the house had been converted into a
station. Now it was furnished without much thought to
comfort with a couple of bulky desks, chairs, and metal

radio equipment. His sneakered feet echoed hollowly around the bare walls.

A sheet of paper wound its way out of the humming fax machine. Cupping his calloused hand under it, he read the message and shook his head. It wasn't going to be easy to find this baby, not easy, but not impossible.

He left the lights on, just swung the door shut, and headed across the short lawn toward the cutter's berth. The government wharf was brightly lit. Not that it mattered; he would know the way with his eyes closed. For the past four years, day in and day out, Danny had beaten a path between the station and the cutter he skippered.

He loved his job. It kept him strong and fit and, most importantly, out on the ocean. Normally he approached each trip with a thrill of adventure tempered with a strong sense of responsibility. Tonight was different. Tonight he was not going to tow in a stranded boat or rescue men from a churning sea. Tonight he was not running the show. The RCMP were.

Along the left side of the wharf a half-dozen silent fishing boats waited, noses toward the shore, for the early morning rush. As he absentmindedly pushed his blond bangs away from his forehead his eyes scanned, checking for anything out of the ordinary.

Chapter Four

Susan, dressed in one of Edna Wilson's slightly pilly sweatsuits, walked down the short hall and into the living room. It seemed like she could still hear the rumble of her kidnappers' fishing boat. Perhaps it was a different one out on the water?

She turned, only to be confronted by a terrifying expanse of picture window. Anyone outside would have a clear view into the cottage. Forcing down her panic, she tried to look beyond her own reflection, but there was too much light behind her. She saw only her own face and the tidy room behind her shoulder—colorful crocheted throws, paintings of sailing ships, wine bottle lamps.

With wobbly legs she crossed the braided carpet to a narrow upholstered chair and sat with its tall back shielding her from the window. Her fingers drummed a staccato beat on the arm. Waiting.

Suddenly she sat bolt upright.

"They're here!" John hollered.

Susan jumped to her feet and circled to the back of the chair.

A deep voice spoke. "I'm sorry it took so long. I was the closest car and I was way over in Spryfield." The Wilsons led the talker into the room.

The RCMP officer inspired confidence as he stood over six feet tall with broad shoulders and a square face. Even his uniform—short-sleeved light-brown shirt, dark blue trousers with a fat gold stripe down the side, black ankle boots, peaked cap, and tie—looked strong and efficient. Reaching inside his blue jacket, he exposed a glimpse of a leather holster. Then he looked at Susan, flipped open a writing pad, and poised his pen.

"You must be Ms. Stead. I'm Constable McCall. Perhaps I could ask you a few questions?"

"This'll take too long. I mean, shouldn't we . . . couldn't you ask them in the car? I think we should be driving over to Amy's house."

"Well, Ms. Stead, the thing to do now is to figure out where the boat's gone so we can update the Coast Guard cutter?" It came out as a question, the last word a notch higher.

"Oh, you're right." She padded, barefoot, from around the chair.

"Okay, I don't know the north, south," she said quickly, pointing this way and that, "but I was on Crescent Beach, far up the right end. The lighthouse was on the left . . . um . . ."

The officer, scribbling in his notebook, asked without raising his head, "How long do you think you were on board with the boat moving offshore?"

"Oh, it felt like forever, but I guess only about five minutes. Once I felt the boat turning, that is. We might have been moving before that; I don't know."

"Did it travel directly out to sea?"

She felt like a terrible witness. "I couldn't say for sure."

"Well, were you traveling away from, or toward the lighthouse?"

"Oh." She closed her eyes and visualized standing on the deck. One hand, fingers straight but tight together, pointed to the front and the other waved over her left shoulder. "The lighthouse was . . . We were going this way and the lighthouse was back there."

He looked at her directly and said calmly, "You're doing fine. Just fine. What type of boat was it?"

"It was a fishing boat, I'm pretty sure of that. It didn't smell fishy though, more like diesel. They didn't have any lights on, not at first. It was pretty big, about as long as the average city driveway—three, maybe four car lengths."

"Did you see any numbers? Name? Markings?"

Susan shook her head no. Her eyes filled and she bit her bottom lip looking from one face to the other. They waited anxiously. She rubbed her hands briskly over her face, welcoming the pain the motion caused her sore jaw.

The constable put his pen inside his jacket. "You keep thinking while I call in this update to the rescue center." He left the room to call, apparently from his car radio.

Susan noticed the condition of her feet—bruised and bloody from the rough trek from the shore. "Mrs. Wilson, could I borrow a pair of old shoes? I'll return them when I bring back the clothes."

Edna looked doubtfully at Susan's size-seven feet. "I wear size five."

John Wilson chimed in. "I'll get you some of my sneakers."

As the RCMP officer returned he said, "Well now, Ms. Stead, perhaps we should see about getting you to a doctor. I know there's a lot more to—"

Susan stopped him. "Oh no, I couldn't. We have to

see Amy's parents." She had a sudden thought. "Where's this rescue center?"

He frowned. "In Dartmouth, but they'll dispatch the *Seal Harbor* cutter. But I don't think you're in any condition—"

"I can rest later. Let's go to the Coast Guard station first. While we're driving I'll try to think of things that might help them."

The Coast Guard cutter *Seal Harbor*—a 44-foot, self-righting lifeboat—had a slicker-yellow superstructure with doors that could be shut and sealed as tight as a submarine. At night the red hull looked black but the tow rope, wound around a giant winch on deck, gleamed white in the moonlight.

Just as Danny stepped on board, he saw the headlights of two cars turn into the parking area. He waited with one hand on the guard railing. The cutter's engines quivered beneath his feet.

" 'Evening, folks." He didn't say anything to the woman who approached with the three Mounties, but he looked her over carefully. She wore a blue sweatsuit. Much too small, it pulled tightly over her narrow hips. Her skin looked soft and pale in the glare of the wharf lights, and her long hair curled wild and uncombed.

Flanked as she was by the burly Mounties, she looked petite, but when he hopped off the boat and up the few steps from the cutter's berth to stand in front of her, he realized that she was only a few inches shorter than his six feet.

She afforded him a quick glance and resumed her intense study of a nearby fishing boat.

He had the impression of blue, red-rimmed eyes that had recently seen horrors—and were still seeing them. She trembled. An angry swelling started at her jaw and spread all the way to her cheekbone. When she sniffed

and swiped at her reddened nose, he had to control the
impulse to take the squall jacket he carried and wrap it
about her stiff shoulders.

Constable McCall, whom he knew slightly, made the
introductions. "Danny Shipley, this is Susan Stead. She's
the woman with the complaint."

Danny reached out a hand to shake hers but she surprised him by pointing to the *Betsy*. Her voice was
hoarse and anxious. "What's that? That thing sticking
out front?"

"It's a swordfish stand." Danny assumed she meant
the iron structure jutting from the bow of the boat. "You
harpoon swordfish off that."

"It had one of those," Susan said breathlessly. She
wrapped her arms around her body and squeezed. "It
could have been that very boat. Has it been here all
night?" She swung her head and looked anxiously down
the dark beach.

"It was here when I left this afternoon," he said as he
walked briskly to the side of the *Betsy*.

She followed him and peered onto the deck. "No, no,
it had big round things"—she held her arms wide—"like
wound-around rope or wire, and the deck was different.
Not so open. I tripped over short walls."

Danny was not discouraged by her stumbling words.
"A herring seiner. They use those winches when they
haul aboard—"

"I don't need a lesson." Susan rounded on him.
"Every second you waste, they're taking Amy farther
away. Go get them!"

She was right, of course, but her tone smarted. He
wanted to apologize because it seemed important that
she liked him, but he knew that his words would be
wasted.

As he swung to leave he heard Susan ask Constable

McCall, "Do you think I can go too? I know what Amy looks like."

"No, ma'am." The RCMP officer's voice was firm. "If they run into a fishing boat like this one, and there's a kid around, they won't need you to identify her."

Once back on board Danny stepped into the bridge to face the instruments. The radar was warmed up, beeping. He watched as Harkey let the lines go, then he wrapped his fingers around the red balls on the ends of each lever—one engine ahead, one astern. He concentrated on the task and seconds later they charged toward the open sea.

There were five men on board—two deckhands, two RCMP officers, and Danny, the skipper.

"Off we go," he said to Mark DeLong, the burly RCMP staff sergeant standing by his side on the cramped bridge.

"Think we'll find them?" DeLong asked, running his hand over the stubble of his salt-and-pepper brush cut.

"Oh yeah. It might take a while but we'll find them." Danny leaned toward the opening to the deck and called back, "Harkey, get the charts out, will ya?"

His gaze continued beyond the stern, across the ever-expanding stretch of water, to the dock. Susan Stead had not moved. She was still on the wharf looking, he thought, at the wharf lights glinting off the cutter's wake.

He dragged his eyes back to the instrument panel and asked, "What's the story with the woman?"

"She says she was on the beach about midnight and caught some guys manhandling a four-year-old girl. She knows the little girl, she says, but she couldn't come up with her last name." He didn't sound convinced. "Anyway, she tried to save the kid and got dragged out to a fishing boat by two guys. One of them claimed, according to the woman, that the others were going to kill her, so he threw her overboard."

"Were they very far out?" Danny asked, concerned for the ordeal she must have suffered. Dropped in the middle of the ocean, at night. . . . Most people would have drowned.

DeLong shrugged. "She had a life jacket."

"Owner's name on it?"

"Nope."

"What about the kidnapping story?"

DeLong changed positions slightly before answering. "It's hard to say. No one claims their kid's gone missing. But it's not like we can ignore the charge. She seems like a credible witness."

Danny remembered the bruise on Susan's face, "Looks like they roughed her up some."

"Or she hit a rock swimming in."

For a moment Danny prodded his bristled, sun-bleached moustache with the tip of his finger and considered DeLong's skepticism. Was it just a policeman's nature to be suspicious? Could that intriguing woman be lying? And if so, why? The cutter cleared the mouth of Seal Harbor and moved out into the channel.

"Decision time. Seems to me, if they were steaming along at eight knots, they could be most anywhere by now." Danny stepped back, keeping a hand on the wheel and sweeping the other in a wide arc. "Sixteen miles that way." He pointed with two fingers like a gun. "Sixteen miles that way. Or sixteen miles that way."

He veered southwest, leaving the Seal Harbor Island Lighthouse slowly turning its beam behind him. "Our way's as good as another," he said, "but there're lots of hiding places around Rogues Roost."

When the second deckhand poked his head through the door to the bridge, Danny said to him, "You and Harkey take over here. We'll go down below and check out the charts. Keep an eye on the radar and see if you can raise them on the radio. Use all the channels. Ask if anyone out there's seen them. We're looking for a herring seiner that's acting weird, no lights or putting in somewhere odd, something like that."

The interior of the cutter was small and functional. There were plastic-covered benches on either side and fire extinguishers and speakers mounted high on the bulkheads. Through another door, deeper inside, were hammocks, squall jackets, life jackets, and folded gray blankets. It was clearly not a pleasure boat.

Staff Sergeant DeLong repeated skeptically, "Raise them on the radio? Come on."

Danny shrugged. "They won't answer if they're up to no good. Then if we see anyone on the radar who looks likely and who hasn't responded . . ." He left the sentence unfinished, paused, and looked at DeLong. "From then on it's your show. Got a plan?"

DeLong patted the holster at his side. "We'll hail them, tell them to heave to, board them, and arrest them." His eyes were humorless. "At least, that's what we do in principle."

"There's a kid on board."

"So the Stead woman says."

"What's to stop them from getting rid of the evidence? What's to stop them from dumping the kid when they realize they're going to get caught?"

"We'll just have to hope they're not so cold-hearted as that."

Danny tried to concentrate on the chart spread before him. Tried but could not. He remembered the haunted look in Susan's eyes and the inflamed bruise on her face. He'd like to get the guys who did that to her. "They tossed the Stead woman overboard," he said grimly.

Staff Sergeant DeLong did not have an answer to that.

Chapter Five

Susan turned to look at the clock on the bedside table. 5 A.M. Muffled street sounds floated up the four stories to her bedroom: a bus picking up speed, a car horn. Her refrigerator clicked on; an elevator hummed.

How could she sleep when she knew that Amy was still missing? Every time she remembered how she'd let that man toss her off the boat, she felt ashamed. She should have stayed on board; she should have stayed with Amy.

She allowed herself a flicker of hope as she visualized the Coast Guard cutter's skipper. Danny Shipley. The Mounties talked about him like he was a local legend. He did look capable, strong and brave, yet sympathetic and understanding. If she had daydreamed for weeks, she couldn't have conceived of a more worthy-looking man to lead the search.

Sure he looked the part, Susan fretted as she squeezed a handful of sheet, but did he have staying power?

25

Would he commit himself to the search? Would he give it his all? He didn't seem in much of a rush the night before but he didn't know the whole story then. Why, perhaps he had already found Amy.

Kicking aside her duvet, she pulled herself painfully into a sitting position. Everything hurt as she forced her stiff muscles to move across the plush gray carpeting and into the bathroom where she lowered onto her knees and reached to turn the white taps of her whirlpool bath.

While the water gurgled and frothed into the tub she leaned one palm on the marble countertop and examined her face in the mirror. No amount of makeup would cover the reddish-purple bruises and swelling.

Abruptly she turned off the taps, wrapped a bath sheet about herself, and went back into the bedroom where she sat on the edge of the bed. On the floor at her feet the telephone book was still open to the number of the RCMP's General Investigation Section because, starving for some word about Amy, she had called them countless times during the night.

She dialed the number again and asked for Staff Sergeant DeLong.

"I'm sorry, he isn't in the office. May I take a message?"

"Could I speak to someone about the kidnapping that happened on Crescent Beach last night? This is Susan Stead."

After a moment another voice broke the silence on the line. "Hello, Ms. Stead, this is Constable McCall."

"Oh, yes." She remembered him from the Wilson's cottage. "Please, did they find her?"

"No, ma'am. I'm sorry. They searched up and down the shoreline until early this morning but didn't have any luck."

"Oh, no. Her poor parents."

"Well"—he dragged out the syllable—"we're not sure we've found the parents."

"But they live in the house above the beach. You were there—I pointed it out when I took you to the spot where it happened." Susan's mind reeled. Locating Amy's parents was critical.

"Yes, ma'am, the one with the big verandah."

"They told me last night that officers would be going to the house. Didn't they go there?"

"Well, yes ma'am, they did. But the occupants of the house say their daughter is fine."

"Fine? How could that be? I saw her with my own eyes."

"There could be a lot of explanations. Perhaps it was a different child, or maybe the men you saw had every right to be there."

"What do you mean, *every right!* Every right to manhandle a little child, every right to hurt me?"

"No," he hedged, "no. I mean that the child may have been a daughter of one of the men."

Susan shook her head. "No, that can't be." Her voice grew more hoarse. "It *was* Amy. They were so rough with her."

"Well, someone was rough with you, that's for sure. Please be assured that we are putting all effort into finding the men who assaulted you."

"But Amy . . . Her parents say she's not missing? They're obviously lying. The kidnappers have warned them to keep quiet. That must be it. Did you or anyone actually see Amy?"

"Well, ma'am, we didn't get a search warrant."

"Did you go to the house yourself?"

"Yes, I did."

"And?"

"They said their child was fine."

"You should have demanded to see her."

He took a moment to reply. "I expect you've had a pretty hard go of it. My advice to you would be to leave this investigation up to us. If that child has been kidnapped, that'll come out in the investigation."

"If? How can you say *if?*"

"As I say"—he ignored her outburst—"there could be a number of explanations for what you saw. Remember, you had to be pretty mixed up yourself. I know it can be scary on the beach late at night. Please try to keep that in mind."

Susan heard the patronizing tone and read between the lines. He thought her wrong, stupid even, to have gone to the beach, all alone, late at night.

"Did they find anything at the spot where it happened?"

"I expect they did. Had it lit up like a stadium."

"And?"

"There was evidence of a scuffle."

"What about the rag? The rag they tried to gag her with must have still been there."

"As I say, they did a thorough search. You can rest assured that everything that can be done, is being done."

After she disconnected, Susan stared at the phone, deep in thought. She had done everything wrong. If only she had hidden when the men brought Amy along the beach. If she had stayed in the shadows and watched, she could have alerted the Coast Guard in time.

All through her bath Susan tried to convince herself that she was not to blame, she was the victim, not the criminal. She scrubbed until her skin flared red but an acid remorse gnawed at her innards.

"Why did I do that?" she cried out loud into the empty room. "Why? How could I have been so stupid?"

Susan knew she couldn't undo the past. The way she was acting smacked of self-pity so she resolved to make amends, to do her best to rescue Amy and return her to her parents. She would offer to help them any way they wanted, as they went through the horrible, horrible ordeal. It was the least she could do.

An hour later Susan's car purred up the graded drive to Amy's hilltop house. She'd decided to go there before heading to her office. She watched the front window and door expecting someone to appear there and wait anxiously until she explained herself. After all, the occupants of the house had to be living a nightmare. But even as she picked her way carefully across the gravel, her high heels sinking into the loose stone, there was no movement from the house.

Susan's heart thudded in her chest as she climbed the wide steps to a heavy door. Her finger stabbed twice at the lit pad. She heard the reverberating bell within the house, followed by a deep silence. No answering shadow moved behind the stained glass window, no muffled voices or twitching curtains. She rang the bell again then turned to study the view.

Far below there was only one car in Crescent Beach's parking lot. After a moment Susan saw its owner, a man running along the sand throwing a stick for a bounding dog. It was an overcast day. Heavy clouds stalled above the earth's surface, hovering but not touching the horizon that stretched its clear, slightly curved line. The water, a deep blue in the distance and greener near shore, rested, broad and alive, like an organic being. Here and there islands sat gray-black on the water. Susan could see puffs of white where the surf crashed on their distant shores.

She followed the course her captor must have traveled the night before, and even as her eyes swept the water she half prayed that a sinister fishing boat would appear.

Still no one answered her ring. She went back down the stairs and along slate blocks delineating the walkway, until she rounded the back of the house. A high chain-link fence surrounded an empty in-ground swimming pool and slate patio area. Expensive-looking cedar furniture, without cushions, was pulled up under an awning in disarray—no cozy sitting arrangements here. A child-sized copy of a lawn chair lay on its side.

Susan shook the heavy padlock hanging from the chain and called anxiously, "Hello? Hello?" She held her hands shoulder height and grabbed onto the wires so tightly that they pressed painfully into her fingers. "Hello? Please, anyone?"

All the long drive from the city she had rehearsed what she would say when she saw Amy's parents. They weren't even home. She noticed for the first time that there were no cars in the driveway or articles of clothing on the clothesline stretched from a corner window. The only sounds were the wind blowing the dry leaves in the trees, crickets chirping, and the haunting cries of circling seagulls.

She returned to her car, opened the door, and leaned the heel of her hand on the horn. Still, when the echo of the blast died, no one came.

She just knew she could not leave it be—she had to do something. She closed her eyes and lived again the feeling of Amy's terrified body tight against hers.

Susan drove around the circular driveway and down the hill. As she stopped at the edge of the pavement, her turning signal clicking, a bicyclist appeared. She put her car in park and jumped out.

"Hello, excuse me?"

He was thin, with greasy jeans, a baseball cap on his head, and an elderly face lined with wrinkles. He skidded one foot on the ground to slow his bike to a halt.

"Excuse me," she repeated, "but do you know the name of the people who live in this house?"

"Sutherland." He did not elaborate.

"Sutherland? Do you know where they've gone? If anyone will be home soon?"

"Nope, don't know 'em myself. He works in the city."

"Ah, well, thank you." She smiled and got back into her car. Sutherland.

For a couple of miles she tooled the narrow road following the twisting coastline, then turned up into Seal Harbor. Leaning forward, her chin almost touching the steering wheel, she watched carefully out the windshield until the red-and-white Coast Guard sign directed her to the right. She swung to a stop on the packed dirt between the red house that housed the station, and the wharves where, the night before, she had stood and watched the cutter steam away.

A man with steel-gray hair and a ruddy complexion dabbed paint in the corner of a white window frame. He greeted Susan with a bright grin.

"Could I speak to the man who was here last night?" she asked.

He held the fat paintbrush up like a sign. "I was here. Will I do?"

"Well, yes, well . . . Ummm . . ." Susan stuttered.

A look of concern wiped the mischievous grin from his face. "I expect you mean the skipper. Come on." He dumped his brush in a tin and elbowed aside the door, calling, "Yo Skipper, there's somebody here to see ya."

He looked different in the daylight, but Susan recognized the man who peered around the corner to be the same one she snapped at the night before. He had a wiry red-blond moustache, unruly blond hair that flopped over his forehead, and a tanned face.

"Do you remember me? I was here last—"

"Sure, Susan, isn't it?"

He crossed to meet her with an outstretched hand that, out of reflex, she shook in her firm, businesslike grip. He did not let it go immediately but studied the bruise on her face. At the same time she anxiously searched his for a sign, but it was immediately apparent from the regret in his gray-blue eyes that he did not have any news about Amy. As her hopes sagged, he dropped her hand.

"Come on in and take a weight off your feet."

She tried not to look at the virile way his body moved in the soft fabric of his uniform. It didn't seem right to find him so attractive at a time like this. Frowning, she sank into the overstuffed chair he indicated while he pulled his wooden seat to face her.

Susan heaved a shuddering sigh. "I was hoping you had some news."

He shook his head. "Sorry. There are so many places for them to hide, so many."

She looked past his broad shoulders through the large, multipaned window to the wharf below. "There were more boats here last night."

"Yup. They got an early start today."

It annoyed her that Danny was openly admiring her legs but she controlled the impulse to pull her tight green skirt further down and wished, fleetingly, that she hadn't dressed for the office.

"The RCMP boys brought their boat around from Halifax this morning. They're out there now, looking." He leaned forward, feet flat, elbows on his knees, and asked, "You okay?"

"It's just that, well, there's got to be something . . . something I can do. I keep thinking about Amy—that's the little girl's name, Amy. She must be so frightened." Her voice caught and she stopped to concentrate on squeezing hard on a pinch of skin on her palm—anything to keep from crying.

"It's not your fault, you know."

"Oh . . ." She dug into her purse for a tissue. "I know it's not."

"Knowing and feeling are two different things, two very different things."

The radio crackled and he tilted his head, listening. Susan, holding her breath, could not make out any of the words spoken but he seemed at ease.

"It's a standard reaction," he continued when the radio was quiet. "You feel like you deserved to be attacked. Victims of violent crime often, heck, *usually* react that way."

His gaze was too intense. The temptation to succumb to his sympathy was great. She had to be strong, and that meant keeping a distance physically as well as mentally. If he touched her again she knew she would burst into tears. But as Susan tried to stand, the soft, enveloping chair defeated her. Her awkward struggling exposed more of her long, silk-clad legs. When she finally gained her feet she felt embarrassed and peeved.

"Can we talk about the search, please?" she snapped without looking him in the eye.

"Well, just so you understand that knowing and feeling are two different things."

"Thank you," she said firmly, "for your concern. But it's Amy we should be discussing."

He shrugged and hopped to his feet. "Listen, can I get you a cup of tea? There's some brewed."

"Coffee?" Susan was not a tea drinker.

He scoffed. "I don't touch the stuff. You'll like this tea. It's jasmine. Herbal tea's a lot better for you."

"Jasmine tea? No thank you."

It was all she could do not to snap at him. He was so lackadaisical about everything.

Danny moved to a vast pale-colored chart tacked to the wall. "This is where we are and this is where we looked last night." He followed his finger along the thin line dividing the blue ocean with the green land.

As she watched him, Susan began to get an indication

of the awesome number of places where the boat could be hiding, assuming it was still in the area. Even if they studied every island and inlet within twenty miles of Seal Harbor, they would be covering only a dozen square inches of the wall-sized chart.

"There has to be a better way," she said. "Are you checking on the boats that were out?"

"You see, it's like this. We"—he jabbed his fingers at his chest—"don't do the investigations. The RCMP do. We don't have power to arrest. We're mainly concerned with safety at sea. That's what we do here, ensure safety at sea. The Coast Guard is actually—"

Susan held up a hand. "I understand that, but don't you know the fishermen? Wouldn't you be able to find out which boats were where last night?"

He hooked two thumbs in the pockets of his trousers and looked out the window. "Yup, we would. We pretty much know all the local boats of any size, you know, if they're from around this way."

A tail of his blue uniform shirt bunched above his belt. As though feeling her eyes on it, Danny jammed it into his pants with his left hand, palm outward. He did not wear a wedding band. The gold lettering on his shoulder patch spelled *Coast Guard Canada, Garde Côtière.*

"Well? Are you going to check?"

"Sure. It doesn't take much, you know. It's a small community; people talk. Something like this is big news. Why, I bet if I picked up that phone now—"

Susan interrupted, "Then why don't you? The way you act, you'd think we were talking about a missing puppy or something! Amy is a real, live kid. She's sweet and funny and spunky and—Get off your rear and do something!"

A steely glint of anger glared in his eyes and she flinched. His countenance remained passive; he didn't even tense, but his eyebrows lowered a fraction over eyes fitted with icy scrutiny. In that instant everything she felt about Danny Shipley changed. Everything. He may have looked laid-back and relaxed, but passion flared in his eyes, passion and pride and grit. He cared. He cared a great deal.

Chapter Six

Dianne, the Sampson Corporation receptionist sitting in siege behind her workstation, did a double take when Susan walked through the door. "What happened to you?"

"It's a long story. If you don't mind, I'd rather not go into it now," Susan said, reaching into her message slot.

"Oh, okay. I'm supposed to tell you the minute you get in that Mr. Moore wants to see you," Dianne said with an apologetic tilt of her head.

Susan did not look up but continued leafing through her pink message slips: Jack from National Sea wanted more mailing labels, a Ms. Jones wanted to know where she could get model 1R4 training, and a John Hayes wanted her to call him.

"Mr. Moore does? Any idea why?" Susan asked when Dianne's comment finally sank in. Gordon Moore, her immediate superior, was a festering thorn in her side— a greedy, pushy sales manager who did not think women had a right to work outside the home much less as sales reps.

"You missed the monthly sales meeting."

"Oh, no, that's right. That was this morning."

Dianne countered Susan's dismay with a dash of determined cheerfulness. "I think that Hayes message is a bluebird. He asked to speak to a sales rep about buying a photocopier."

Susan glanced at the slip again. A bluebird—a sale made out of the blue over the telephone—would be a nice change. Lately, she had been scrambling for every new customer. "I hope so," she replied.

Sales reps rarely ventured inside the Sampson offices during the day. According to the Powers That Be, sales were not made by sitting at a desk. But Susan needed to see a friendly face, so she asked hopefully, "Anyone else in?"

"Nope, all out on calls."

She smiled a thanks to Dianne before punching, with a stiff middle finger, the security code on the inner door key pad. Then, hearing the faint clicking sound of the tumblers opening, she pulled it wide.

Gordon Moore glared at her from across a large, open area filled with desks and file cabinets, but no other people. The room was known as the bullpen. Susan preferred to call it the playpen, a term more in keeping with the atmosphere at the end of the day when her fellow sales representatives returned from pounding the pavement.

"Well, well, well, look who decided to pay us a visit," he said with a sneer.

She didn't answer until she stood a few steps from him and placed her briefcase on the top of her desk. "I'm sorry I missed the meeting this morning." When she saw he eyed her without sympathy Susan remembered her bruised face and turned it away. "Anything happen I should know about?"

"You missed a very productive meeting." He ran a hand over his short red hair.

"I wish I'd been able to be there."

"Well, you should have at least called in. We waited for you. Time is money, Susan. Well? Do you think you can just turn up at lunchtime without an explanation? Well, do you?"

He hovered there, an expectant expression on his flushed face, but Susan made an elaborate show of setting out her messages in a straight line, then picked up the telephone. Gordon Moore stamped off before she had finished dialing the first number, so she pressed a trembling finger on the button and listened to the dial tone.

Generally speaking, she reminded herself, Gordon Moore had no cause to complain. She was one of his top sales representatives; in fact she had won the coveted President's Club trip for outstanding sales figures during the two previous years. Customers trusted her and came back to her time and again. She did not make a habit of missing meetings.

Her eyes skimmed the posters tacked in regimental form around the room: photocopiers, word processors, computers, fax machines, postage machines, adding machines—the model numbers sounded like high-powered foreign cars. Despite past hours of effectively pitching such machinery, today she could not drum up any enthusiasm.

She was tired and sore, worried and anxious. Was it only three days ago that she had sat at this very desk laughing and joking with Chuck, Ray, Lew, and the others? *Boy,* she thought to herself, *what a difference a weekend can make.*

Reaching for the phone she dialed, from memory, the RCMP office.

"CID, Staff Sergeant DeLong speaking."

"This is Susan Stead. I wondered if you've had any news on Amy Sutherland?"

"No, ma'am," he answered in a bored voice.

"Can you tell me what's happening?"

"CID is currently investigating the matter."

"I know that, but—"

"Excuse me, ma'am, but perhaps you could give me a number where you can be reached during the day? I'll call you if we have any developments."

Susan had filled out all the forms at the Halifax Detachment of the RCMP the night before and she knew DeLong was aware of that, but she played his charade and repeated the numbers.

After she hung up, Susan groaned and chewed on her knuckle. The waiting, not knowing, was intolerable. She had to do something to help Amy!

She snatched her briefcase, rushed across the bullpen, and, with an abrupt wave to Dianne, hurried from the Sampson Building. A strong wind funneled between the towering office buildings lining Hollis Street. It forced her to walk at a cant, her face averted from the swirling dust. She moved purposefully. With long strides she passed men in three-piece suits and women holding their skirts close to their legs and safe from the gusts, then she slowed her step while a white Halifax Transit bus, spewing black diesel fumes, plodded past. She crossed the street against the light and climbed ancient stone steps.

As the plate-glass doors whooshed closed behind her, the traffic sounds were replaced by telephones ringing and voices humming. She ignored the questioning looks from the receptionist and headed straight for Marty Sherman's desk.

He did not see her at first; he stared at the ticker-tape display at the ceiling, reading, analyzing the stock market. His hair was freshly buzzed close to his head and he wore his customary uniform—white shirt, bow tie, and gray suit. His paunch had swelled since she last saw him.

"What's a girl gotta do to buy some stocks and bonds around here?" With one hand on her hip, she feigned an indignant voice.

"Susan! What a nice surprise!" He jumped out of his seat and advanced, arms wide for a hug, but stopped in mid-stride. "What happened to you? Walk into a door?"

"I got beat up," she answered simply.

"No!" His eyes were sober, watching her as she sat down. "You want to tell me about it?"

"Sure. Got caught up in a kidnapping, was punched, kidnapped, and thrown overboard. Nothing really," she said with a smile to soften the sarcastic words.

Then she became serious and related the whole story. She did not put voice to the emotional turmoil. The pain was still too close to the surface. He listened silently, his hands cupping his knees, leaning forward, eyebrows lowered. When she finished he pulled her from her seat and gave her a huge, rocking hug.

"Phew!" He shook his head. "That's a lot to take in. You poor kid!"

"Oh, I'll live." She winced at her stiff muscles when she sat down again.

"So you spent the night with the Mounties?"

"Pretty much," Susan agreed. "We went to Seal Harbor first, and I told the Coast Guard skipper what I could. He took the Mounties out on his boat."

"Well, you know what they say, the Mounties always get their man."

Susan shrugged and shook her head.

Marty squeezed her hand and said, "They're good men."

"I know, but, well . . ." For a moment Susan struggled

to make sense of her confused emotions. "I feel kind of connected with Amy, somehow part of it, yet I'm so helpless. Do you know what I mean?"

"You want to catch the bad guys," Marty said.

"I've got to do something!"

"Sure you do. You're an intelligent woman. No reason why you shouldn't do a little investigating on your own." He leaned forward, his eyebrows lowered. "You've got a perfect cover, so no one will suspect you."

"As a Sampson employee, you mean. I've thought of that. But the problem is, what if . . . ? They said that Amy had to be kept alive until next week."

"Oh, no! Are you sure it wasn't bravado? Do you think they might have been trying to frighten you?"

Susan snickered ruefully. "They succeeded." After a deep breath, she continued, "It's possible. I've got to find out why they took her in the first place."

"Ransom jumps to mind."

"Considering where she lives, I have to believe Amy's family has money."

"The Mounties have probably got that covered. What's this Coast Guard chap like?"

She was amazed how clearly Danny Shipley's face appeared in her memory. "At first I didn't think he was interested in helping—he said that it wasn't his job— but now I don't know. You know how some country people act slow and unconcerned but really they're sharp thinkers?"

"Sure. It's just a mannerism. Everyone in Seal Harbor talks that way."

After a moment he leaned back and said in an expansive voice, "So, what can I do to help?"

"I need some information. Those people, the Sutherlands, what do you know about them? They must have some connection to the stocks."

"I'll check the bible." He rolled his chair across the

flat carpet and reached in a beige metal credenza. A directory, four inches thick, landed on his desk with a thud.

"Sutherland . . . Sutherland," he mumbled as his fat thumb flipped through the pages. "Right! I thought I knew the name." He slapped the book shut. "I don't even need to read that. His name's in all the papers these days. Robert Sutherland, Chief Executive Officer of CNR, Canada Natural Resources. I've got last year's annual report somewhere here." The end of his sentence was muffled because his head was buried in a file drawer.

"Here, you can keep it, no one's going to need these anymore."

She took the glossy folder and studied its cover—a photograph of navy-blue water with a massive deep-sea oil rig in the distance.

"Oh, I remember now. CNR, that's one of the Crown Corporations that's being privatized."

"Right. Our new Premier's pet project: budget constraints, belt-tightening time, sell off our resources to the highest bidder."

"So Robert Sutherland will be out of a job soon?"

"Would you believe next week?" He shook his head at her confused look. "Don't you ever read the newspapers? CORE is this week. The politicians aren't going to let a chance go by to pat themselves on the back. You know what CORE is?"

"Canadian Offshore Resources Exhibition. Sampson Corp. has a booth rented," Susan said, remembering the fancy dodging she did to avoid being scheduled to work over the weekend manning the Sampson booth.

"You going?"

"Wasn't intending to."

"If you do, you'll have front-row seats to Sutherland's swan song," he said. "The last day of CORE, they're going to announce the winners of the bids."

"Bids for what?"

"Exploration licenses, mineral rights," he said with a shrug.

"What do you mean, exploration licenses?"

"Well, there are gold discoveries. CNR holds the licenses to explore and mine in a number of places. But mostly what we're talking about is oil and gas—offshore oil like the kind under the Scotia Shelf."

"The right to explore there?"

"It's the rights to sink drills into blocks of land under the ocean, mostly around Sable Island," he explained. "There's big government money available for anyone who wants to take the time to find the stuff. After a discovery they bring in partners and go into production."

Susan flipped through the annual report, stopping at a sheet of figures. "Whoa! Look at this," she said. "Their assets last year were worth over two hundred million dollars. Oh wow! Now I know where our tax money's gone, to Petroleum Incentives Program grants—eighty-seven million. Oil and gas properties—twenty-five million. Mineral properties—twenty million." She lowered the folder and stared unseeingly at a blank wall.

"Big money," Marty agreed. "Think this is connected to your little girl's kidnapping?"

"I have no idea. The timing is so obvious. CORE ends on Sunday—the one-week deadline fits." Susan winced at her choice of words, then pulled her briefcase on her lap, flipped it open, and slid the annual report inside. "Thanks, this is good information. I'm going to pay a visit to CNR."

"You watch yourself." He waved an index finger at her. "Who knows what's going on, what kind of people are mixed up in this."

Chapter Seven

As Susan stepped from the elevator her eyes fixed on the heavy bronze letters that glowed dimly on the embossed wallpaper; CNR. From the outside Canadian Natural Resources didn't look like it teetered on the brink of extinction. Her chest felt constricted, as though she was about to take an exam. Why was she so frightened? She didn't even know if she was going to the right office, if this was the right Sutherland! And even if it was, he probably wasn't there. Would *she* be, if her child had been kidnapped? No.

Although the receptionist eyed Susan expectantly as the weighty glass doors hissed closed behind her, she continued talking on the phone. A glass-top coffee table, magazines fanned on its surface, sat in front of a leather couch and chair. Framed photographs, mostly of oil rigs and helicopters, covered the walls. She stepped closer to a striking picture of a man's back. He looked to be examining a pale-colored vein of ore that cut across the face of a wall of rock. The color reflected from the light on his hard hat gleamed like gold.

"May I help you?" the receptionist asked.

"Yes." Susan forced a professional smile and placed her business card face up on the desk. "I'm Susan Stead. If Mr. Sutherland has a moment I'd like to see him about the Sampson equipment." A bold-faced lie, but better to be subtle where Amy was concerned.

The woman picked up the card and, at the same time, dialed a couple of numbers on her phone. "Hi, Mary," she said. "There's a Sampson rep here. Do you want to . . . ? Okay." She hung up without saying good-bye.

"Follow this hall." She pointed. "The first desk is Mr. Sutherland's assistant. She'll help you."

"But is Mr. Sutherland in?"

"You'll have to speak to his assistant."

Susan's feet felt like lead because, from the receptionist's words, she gathered that Sutherland was in. Did that mean he was the wrong man? Surely someone would not go to work the day after his daughter had been kidnapped.

"Hello, I'm Mary MacDonald." A capable-looking woman in her late thirties came from behind a desk. She had strands of gray in the dark hair at her temples and wore a severe navy suit.

Susan introduced herself, then asked, "Is Mr. Sutherland available to see me?"

Administrative assistants, like executive secretaries, were often bastions protecting The Boss's time. Susan knew from experience that the best way to bypass them was to remain friendly but aloof, professional but slightly impatient, and, above all, closemouthed about the nature of her business with The Boss.

"What is this in relation to?" Mary tried. She seemed to be looking more at Susan's bruises than her eyes.

By way of an answer, Susan handed over a business card.

"Is it anything I can help you with?" Mary persisted.

"No. Thank you." Susan raised her eyebrows and pasted a closed-lipped smile on her face.

"Mr. Sutherland is a very busy man. I generally handle the administration matters of the office."

"I realize that, but we're talking about a lot of valuable Sampson equipment. I know he'll want to talk to me. It's important."

After a hesitation, Mary turned her back on Susan to speak quietly into her phone. Presumably she was told to allow Susan in because, after hanging up, she led her to tall, mahogany doors.

"Mr. Sutherland, this is Ms. Stead from Sampson."

Susan took a few steps into the office and the door closed softly behind her. She was alone with Robert Sutherland.

He did not turn to welcome her. Instead he appeared to be looking out the floor-to-ceiling corner window, up the Halifax Harbor toward McNabs Island and the Atlantic Ocean. He wore a gray suit. The jacket crinkled in the back because his hands were shoved into the pockets of his slacks. His shoulders were rigid.

After a long minute Susan asked softly, "Mr. Sutherland?" When he turned and she saw his receding hairline and steel-gray hair, she was assailed by doubt. This could not be Amy's father; he was too old.

He seemed surprised that he wasn't alone. The vacant look cleared from his eyes; he patted down his suit jacket and moved behind his desk.

"What can I do for you, young lady?" he asked in a deep, resonant voice.

"Umm, I'm from Sampson Corporation." Susan was at a loss. Her eyes darted around—anything to avoid looking directly at him—and fell upon a line of family photographs standing on a bookcase. She caught her breath and half-stumbled toward them.

"Oh . . . oh . . ." She faltered, suddenly close to tears. "There's Amy." It was a studio picture, with forced smiles, blurred curtains in the background. Although Amy sat on her mother's lap, they hardly seemed to touch.

He materialized at her side. "You know my daughter?" His voice was hard.

"We're kind of chums, on the beach, you know? She always comes over. . ." She tried to keep still but her instinct was to step backward. He was unapproachable, hard and remote. She found to her dismay that she did not trust Amy's father.

Robert Sutherland reached in front of Susan and picked the picture up. "Do you know my wife too?" he asked.

"No, I don't know her."

"She wasn't on the beach too?" His voice was like ice.

Susan blanched. Was she inadvertently stepping into a family argument? She remembered the way Amy always seemed abandoned there on the beach with her plastic shovel and pail. "I've only seen her when she came to fetch Amy."

He slowly moved his eyes from her face to the picture. Then, still holding it, he returned to his chair.

Susan turned back to the shelf and the remaining photographs. There was another studio picture of two teen-agers—crew-cut hair, crisp shirts unbuttoned at the collar. "Who are these boys?" she asked.

"My sons, from my first marriage."

Still at a loss as to how to approach him, Susan stalled. "They're good-looking boys."

"What can I do for you today?" He started busily shuffling papers about his desk, eyeing her suspiciously.

"Well, actually I came to talk to you about Amy."

His motions froze. "What about her?"

There was no good way to say it. "I saw her being kidnapped." Susan's words hung in the air. "Last night. I was on the beach when it happened."

Robert Sutherland narrowed his eyes. A muscle tightened and relaxed in his jaw. "What did you say?"

Susan rushed on. "Last night I was on the beach and I saw two men take Amy. They took her on a fishing boat. Is she okay? Have you heard anything? Please tell me what's going on. I feel so badly that I—"

"What are you blathering about!" he shouted.

"I know I'm babbling. I'm sorry." She straightened, annoyed at her loss of composure. "You can talk to me, you know, openly. I'm not the police. That is, they, the kidnappers, probably told you not to talk to the police?"

Sutherland said nothing, but his face seethed in anger.

Susan tried again to reach him. "I want you to know, Mr. Sutherland, that I will do anything within my power to help you get Amy back."

He curled his lip. "I don't know what you're talking about. My stepdaughter is fine. I ate breakfast with her this morning!" The last word came out as a bellow.

Susan's mouth hung open. She felt nailed to the floor even when he advanced on her menacingly.

"Get out!" He snatched her discarded briefcase and slapped it into her arms.

Suddenly the administrative assistant had the door held wide and Susan stumbled past. "But Amy?" she kept asking. "Amy's all right? They let her go?"

When she finally gained her balance, Susan stopped and turned toward Sutherland. He shut the door in her face.

Susan staggered to a nearby file cabinet and clutched it until the trembling in her knees stilled. She was dimly aware that Sutherland's assistant hovered nearby.

"What was that all about?" Mary asked in a whisper.

"I'm sorry," she mumbled. "It was a personal matter. I was misinformed, or something."

"Can you tell me about it?"

"No, it's personal."

"Well." Mary moved away from the office door toward the exit and motioned for Susan to follow. "It might help to talk about it."

"Thank you." Susan heaved a shuddering sigh. "But believe me, it wouldn't help."

"Well, I see." She added confidentially, "You have to excuse Mr. Sutherland; he's under tremendous pressure these days." They had reached the glass exit doors when she said, "Why don't you go somewhere and have a nice cup of tea? There's a spot downstairs, you know."

Susan smiled weakly at her kindness and nodded a good-bye.

Still shaken, she leaned her hand on the elevator button, and by the time the doors slid open to the expansive foyer on the ground level, the shock had started to lift. Robert Sutherland had said that he had breakfast with Amy, and that she was not missing. Did she believe him?

She crossed the lobby and entered a small restaurant. It was designed for the coffee break and lunch crowd—high-backed booths around the outer walls and a long, U-shaped counter up the middle. She perched on a stool and dropped her briefcase on the floor at her feet, then ordered a cup of coffee from the waitress who looked after customers from her long narrow station between the parallel counters.

For ten minutes, she tried to understand Sutherland's attitude. There was no doubt in her mind that Robert Sutherland's daughter had been kidnapped. So, what did that mean? Was the child taken and returned without her father being aware? Perhaps he didn't spend the night at home. Perhaps no one told him. But he said he had eaten breakfast with her?

The waitress came by and asked Susan if she wanted a refill. While she was pouring the brew the restaurant door opened. Although Susan saw the waitress's hand arrest over the mug as she eyed the newcomers, Susan did not see the men herself until they walked all the way around the U of the counter to sit exactly opposite her.

They looked out of place in an office tower restaurant: blue jeans, greasy hair, dirty fingernails. One wore a red-and-black checked jacket and the other a green quilted vest. But it was not their attire that made Susan's skin crawl. They both stared at her with silent, angry contempt. She tried to look away but her eyes kept darting back to them.

"Two coffees," one man barked at the waitress without taking his cold gaze from Susan's face.

Her immediate thought was that her professional attire and briefcase outraged the strangers. Some men resented businesswomen indiscriminately. But she had never been singled out in such an obvious manner.

Finally Susan asked, "Is there a problem?"

The man in the vest turned up his lips in a sneering smile. "Why, Ms. Stead." He clearly enjoyed her shocked expression. "What makes you think something's the matter?"

Susan studied their faces. "Do I know you?" They did look vaguely familiar.

His friend snickered. "You will, if you're not real careful."

Susan's nostrils flared. "What do you mean by that? How do you know my name?"

The two silently contorted their faces into angry masks and glowered at her.

"Are you threatening me?"

Nothing. She slapped a one-dollar coin on the table, slid off her stool, and stomped away. The back of her neck twitched.

Chapter Eight

While Susan waited impatiently to be connected to the Criminal Investigations Division of the RCMP, two of her friends and coworkers, Chuck Wolff and Lew Cox, strolled into the bullpen.

"Yo! Susan!" Chuck bellowed across the room. "What's happening?"

She covered the mouthpiece and answered, "Hi guys, gimme a sec here."

A voice crackled in her ear. "CID, Staff Sergeant DeLong speaking."

Susan abruptly turned away from Lew and Chuck. "Hello, this is Susan Stead. I know you told me you would call if you heard anything new, but I've got some information for you."

"With regard to what?"

"The kidnapping last night! Don't tell me you've forgotten my name already."

"No, ma'am, my mind was on something else when you announced yourself. What can I do for you?"

Susan willed herself to relax. "I've just spoken to Amy's father. His name is Sutherland—Robert Sutherland—and he works at the Canadian Natural Resources office."

"Miss Stead, we spoke to the man last night. I don't suppose he changed his story for you?"

"Well, he claimed that Amy wasn't kidnapped," she admitted. "But that doesn't mean anything. Of course he'd say that if he'd been warned to keep his mouth shut."

"So that's it?"

"No. After I left his office I went downstairs to the lunch counter for a coffee. These two thugs came in and sort of warned me to lay off."

"How so?"

"Well, they didn't say too much, but they knew my name and said if I didn't watch out I'd see more of them."

"Did they specifically mention Sutherland?"

"Well, no. But I'd just left his office not fifteen minutes before that."

For a moment Susan listened to only silence on the earpiece. Finally he said, "Well, Ms. Stead, I suggest you take their advice."

"What! Let them bully me?"

"No, ma'am, keep away from Robert Sutherland. Whether or not his daughter has been kidnapped, the man doesn't want you harassing him."

Appalled, Susan cried, "I wasn't harassing him! I was trying to help."

"The point I'm making, Ms. Stead, is that regardless of how you feel about your ordeal, it's over. We do the investigating. Your job is to try to put all this behind you."

She almost softened at his tone. "I'd love to put it behind me, but all I can do is think about Amy."

"We don't know that there's anything wrong with that child."

"I was there, remember? She was kidnapped."

"Not according to her parents. I'll tell you the way we see it, we're going after the guys who assaulted you. And I want you to know there's a lot of manpower involved in the investigation. You just put all this behind you. Okay?"

"Can't you demand to see Amy? They can't produce her. Will that be proof enough?"

"The child is away with relatives."

"You can get someone to check their story? Go to wherever they claim she's visiting?"

"I'm not going to argue with you, Ms. Stead. I'll call you if I hear anything," he said.

After a defeated-sounding sigh, Susan enunciated carefully, "Thank you, Sergeant."

Susan stared at her hand still clutching the replaced receiver, and ground her teeth.

Lew was watching her with a concerned expression on his face. "You okay?"

Because his concern made her feel weepy, she decided she couldn't talk about it just yet. "Oh, it's nothing. Looks worse than it feels." She saw Lew and Chuck exchange a glance. "Forget it." She shrugged. "So how'd you guys do today?"

"Paper, couple of leads . . ." Lew rolled his eyes and jammed his hands in his pockets. Not a very successful day sale-wise.

Chuck stood, swaggered, pushed his tongue until it bulged in his cheek, and bragged, "I got ink to paper." He paused for effect. "Twice."

She knew he meant that he had two signed contracts. "Well, great! What'd you get?"

"Coby signed the 2024 photocopier, and I sold a new postage meter to Scotia Tire. How about you?"

Susan scoffed, "Don't ask."

"Well, pack up. Lew and I'll buy you a drink at happy hour. You can cry on our shoulders."

"Thanks guys, but all I want right now is a hot bath and bed."

They walked arm in arm to the top of the escalators leading to the street. She smiled gratefully when they left her without pressing about the bruises on her face.

Striding through the pedway, whisking past the Scotia Square fountain and into the grungy parking garage stairwell, Susan was indifferent to her surroundings. Even though she had had to park on an upper level—her late arrival had coincided with the shoppers—she bypassed the empty elevator and trudged up the iron steps. Her heels echoed on the grates. She suddenly realized that the sound was mingling with the heavy tread of at least two people. Susan stopped and listened intently. The scuffing, grating noise came closer.

Tightly squeezing the handle of her briefcase, she tried to tell herself there was no reason to be apprehensive; she had plodded around this place alone countless times with no mishaps. Then her face started to throb and she was assailed with a mental image of the goons who threatened her in the coffee shop. With a blast of energy she sprang up the next two levels and burst through the doors.

The dimly lit field of gray cement stretched empty except for the supporting pillars and a few cars. She ran, her heels clicking, toward her car. Her keys were in the briefcase so she dropped it on the car's hood and struggled with the catches. *Oh, no!* The stairwell doors opened.

Before they could see her, she hunkered down behind her car and held her breath. The steps still approached. Slowly she lowered herself to all fours and peered under the car at the two pairs of feet—high heels and loafers. She dropped her chin on her chest in relief. This was not the usual footwear for goons in red-and-black plaid jackets.

Shaking her head at her own cowardice, she stood, wiped the oil and grit from her knees and hands, collected the keys, unlocked the car door, and threw her briefcase inside. Before starting the engine, however, she checked the floor behind her seat and snapped down the door locks.

Chapter Nine

S usan kept her eyes on the road and ignored the shabby houses, rundown businesses, and miles of scrubby bushes that were brown and limp in the damp fall air. Only the last few miles of the forty-minute drive to Seal Harbor could be called scenic. At the first sign of salt water through the lingering fog, she rolled down her window and breathed deeply. It was important to be calm and relaxed when she reached the Sutherland house.

According to what Mary told her the previous day, Robert Sutherland arrived at the office at 8:00 in the morning, so Susan hoped to find his wife, Deidra, alone. Surely she would listen even if her husband would not. Also, if Amy had not yet been returned, Deidra Sutherland would be at her wits' end and Susan might be able to help with moral support if nothing else.

She allowed herself a moment to daydream, to imagine turning into the driveway and seeing Amy playing happily on the front porch. She'd just drive off then, she told herself. However, when she did pull up the long gravel approach, the house looked as uninhabited as it had two days earlier. There was no telltale twitching curtains or opening door. However, there was a luxury car parked in front of the sprawling garage.

This time Susan walked right around to the swimming pool. The place still looked deserted but the metal gate hung slightly ajar, its open padlock hooked on the latch. When she tugged it wide enough to enter, the hinges creaked like a massive tree bough splitting from its trunk in a storm. One side of the patio doors had been left open and the damp fall breeze stirred the curtains. With a full view of the interior, Susan felt like a peeping Tom. She was looking in at a den with dark wood on the walls, a high bar with rows of liquor bottles, a leather sofa, and two chairs. The tartan pattern of the indoor-outdoor carpet was darkened where the rain had wafted inside.

Susan rapped her knuckles hard on the glass. The wind outside whistled loudly. She knocked again. Nothing.

"Hello?" Susan called, with her face in the opening of the door. She heard a faint sound. Seconds dawdled by, but no one came. "Hello?" she called again, and banged the door until her knuckles smarted. She was not going away this time. Not when she knew there was someone inside.

"Go away!" The distinct words came from the direction of the dark leather chair that faced away.

"Mrs. Sutherland?" Susan asked.

A pale arm flopped over the side of the chair, startling Susan. Manicured fingernails at the end of the arm waved in an impatient beckoning motion. Susan stepped gingerly into the room and around in front of the chair.

She recognized this bleary-eyed woman with her head lolling as Amy's mother.

"Oh, Mrs. Sutherland," Susan gushed. "Are you all right?" She stopped herself before adding, "you poor woman." A puffy-skinned, pitiful creature now replaced the tight-skinned beauty she had seen on the beach.

"Who are you?" Deidra Sutherland asked thickly.

"My name is Susan Stead. Did your husband tell you I went to see him?"

"You!" The word was spoken with such vehemence that Deidra's head bounced against the chair back. Her hands gripped the arms and she glared at Susan through bloodshot eyes.

"I've done nothing wrong! I just want to help. Why are you mad at me?" She suddenly felt ashamed. The woman was obviously distraught. "Look, have you heard anything yet? Has there been a ransom note? Anything?"

"Who are you?" The smell of rum hung heavy in the air.

Susan began slowly, "I'm the person who saw the kidnapping. Didn't your—"

"I know! Who do you think you are, barging in here!"

Susan felt exasperated. "What is the matter with you people? I didn't want to get involved, but I am. Okay? So talk to me, why don't you? Where is Amy?"

Deidra Sutherland appeared to digest Susan's outburst. She dropped her hand to a nearby coffee table, grasped a tumbler half full of amber liquid, and drained it in one gulp. "I can't . . . I'm not talking to you," she slurred.

"Why not? Perhaps I can help, maybe between us?"

Deidra interrupted, "No."

"No because you've been told not to? Or no because you don't want to?"

Deidra averted her face and shook her head.

"But why? I'm not going to do anything that could harm Amy. I promise."

Susan took a step toward Deidra's averted face. Suddenly the woman yawned and pulled a woven blanket up to her chin. "Go away."

"Please." With her heart thumping loudly in her chest, Susan waited, tensed, for a long time. "Mrs. Sutherland?" She moved closer. Deidra was passed out. There was a frayed teddy bear tucked under her elbow.

Both of Amy's parents were determined to keep her away—but why? Maybe they were into something criminal themselves. Or perhaps the kidnappers told them that she would be snooping around and warned them to send her packing.

Susan angrily gritted her teeth. They were not doing anything to find their daughter, at least not as far as she could tell. How could the mother of that beautiful child lie around drunk at a time like this? Susan had to ask herself what she would do in a similar situation. If all she could do was wait, perhaps she would drown her sorrows too.

The kidnappers had said that they had to keep the child alive until next week. So presumably Amy would be held until whatever was going to happen took place. It didn't do any good to imagine the worst. She had to believe someone was looking after the child. Not everyone aboard the boat that night was evil. The man who threw her over the side did so because he didn't want her killed. He wasn't totally bad. She prayed that he would look after the frightened four-year-old.

Susan drove to the Seal Harbor Coast Guard station house. She had barely slammed her car door shut when she heard her name shouted over the haunting cries of the seagulls.

"Susan." Danny Shipley waved from the porch.

He wore his summer uniform, blue short-sleeved shirt and beige trousers. Even at this distance Susan could see the fuzz of hair on his forearm and in the neck of his shirt. His unruly blond bangs fell across his forehead and the wiry moustache curled over his upper lip.

He looked so sincere in his welcome that she waved back and almost bounded up the path. Her smile shriveled into an embarrassed grimace when she reached his side. His eyes twinkled as though he knew she was anxious to see him even before she knew it herself.

"You're an early-bird type, eh?" He grinned. "Got a pot of mint tea steeped—oops, almost forgot, you're a coffee drinker."

As soon as they stepped inside, Harkey, the gray-haired deckhand she had seen on Sunday, piped up, "Just ignore him and his health-food junk. The rest of us drink the real stuff."

Susan smiled. "I'd love a cup. Black. Thanks."

Danny kidded good-naturedly, "You guys'll rot your innards out."

Once again, Susan settled into the soft armchair but it did not defeat her as it had before. This time Danny would have to look at her face and not her legs because she had the foresight to wear a pantsuit and low-heeled shoes.

Danny sat on the wooden chair opposite her. "What's up?"

"I've just come from Amy Sutherland's house. Let's just say no one welcomed me."

"So the little girl's still missing?"

"I think so. I believe her parents have been warned not to talk to anybody." She filled them in on her last couple of days, speaking loudly enough for Harkey to hear from the kitchen.

"This is probably really arrogant of me," she said, "but I feel like I have to try to find Amy because no one else seems to be trying."

Danny responded in his slow, patient voice. "Well, we don't know what's going on behind the scenes. Do you think that Deidra Sutherland would be drunk if there was something she could be doing?"

"I don't know the woman but I do know that I didn't get the feeling that she was the world's best mother." Susan's hand flew to her face, "Oh, what a terrible thing to say! I mean, she just lets Amy wander around that beach with all those strangers. She's only four years old."

Danny stopped toying with his moustache. "I asked around about Amy and she and her mom do live with Robert Sutherland. Diedre's his second wife. They say she's quite a looker."

Susan remembered her booze-ravaged face. "She usually is."

Harkey handed Susan a mug of coffee. "We've been talking about it around here and we figure someone's holding that little girl for ransom. Sutherland's got lots of money," he said as he seated himself on the edge of a desk.

"I'm so relieved you believe me," Susan said. Her eyes felt weepy again so she wrapped two hands around her coffee mug and took a long sip. This weepy side of her personality was unusual and unwelcome. Maybe she hadn't recovered from the physical aspects of her ordeal yet.

The radio crackled. Like the other time she was there, Susan could not make out the words but Danny and Harkey seemed to be tuned to its sound. As soon as the fuzzy mumbling stopped they acted as though there had been no interruption.

Danny said, "I talked to some folks who were walking past the house and saw all three of the Sutherlands just after sunset on Sunday night. But I didn't find anyone who saw anything or anyone around there after that."

Susan felt a wave of gratitude for Danny. "Have the Mounties said anything to you?"

"Naw. As far as we can tell, they've given up." Danny shook his head. "Given up. We took the cutter out and tooled around the islands yesterday. Didn't see anything."

Susan decided that the habit Danny had of repeating things he said was endearing. "I don't know what to do next."

"Well," Danny started. He glanced at Harkey. "We know this guy you might want to be talking to."

"Who?"

"Rummy Smith. He lives on a boat a little ways down the shore. I'll take you over."

"When?" Susan asked anxiously.

"Well, I guess we could go now." He turned to Harkey. "You'll mind the shop, eh?"

"Sure. Got your beeper?"

Danny patted the bulge in the chest pocket of his uniform shirt. "We won't be long."

As Susan struggled out of the deep chair, Harkey warned her about Rummy. "Don't take any drinks from him without watching what he puts into it. Especially coffee."

"Rummy likes his rum," Danny explained.

"I should have guessed."

Rummy didn't live far from the station house, but the route took them along the jagged shoreline up a short lane, around container boxes dropped haphazardly here and there, and along roads that went right through the yards of modern-looking bungalows. Because Seal Harbor had started its existence as a fishing village, people had built their houses where it was convenient to the water, or on their parents' land, or wherever there was a crevice between the giant granite boulders strewn about.

When they neared a fish plant, a sickening stench of fish, brine, diesel, and tar assailed her nostrils. It reminded her of her childhood. She frowned, trying to capture the memory that the smell recalled.

"Something wrong?"

She gave her head a little shake. "I was just remembering something that happened around here, when I was a kid."

"You didn't live around here, did you? I'd have known you if you did."

"No. We just visited for summer holidays. My grandparents used to live up the shore a ways. My great-aunt still lives in Seal Harbor Retirement Village."

"You didn't enjoy those holidays?"

"Oh, I did, I sure did. Some of my happiest memories are . . . were when we played. . . ." As her voice trailed off, she swung an arm to encompass the town and harbor.

"So, what happened? What were you remembering?"

"Nothing. Just one of those little wisps of memory," she said, tugging him forward.

"A good one, or bad one?"

"Good, I think. We had an old rowboat that we used to play in, pretending we were pirates." She smiled at the memory.

"This is a good place for kids," he agreed.

"Not for adults?"

He lifted one shoulder in a shrug. "It is for me. I've lived other places, but this is home. Where else could I get paid to do what I love? Where else?"

"What other places did you live?"

"Went to university in Guelph and then later at Dalhousie."

So he'd lived in both Ontario and Halifax. She wondered what he'd studied but by then they'd reached the public wharves. As they walked toward it, Rummy Smith's home looked cold and foreboding in the overcast light. It was a sixty-foot-long, narrow speedboat with square, block-like superstructures on the deck—quite different from the rounded edges of the nearby fishing boats. The hull, a dark wood, looked as though the clear protective coating had dried and slivered. But the dark green paint on the exterior of the cabins covered smoothly and the bronze around the ports and door hinges was free from mold. The name, *Jacques II,* was printed neatly on the aft.

"He lives on that?" Susan asked, eying the oily water lapping at its hull.

"Yep, yup. It's better inside."

The tide was high so the deck was only a short hop from the wharf, but Danny motioned for her to wait. He crouched opposite a porthole and called, "Ahoy, Rummy Smith."

An aft door cracked open and a voice barked, "Who is it?"

"It's Danny Shipley."

A boot kicked the door open wide. "Well, come in then."

Danny hopped aboard first, then reached for Susan. He clasped her hand firmly and, even when she leaned toward him, the angle of his strong arm did not change. The heat from his skin seemed to travel up her arm and into her chest. She didn't want to let go of that warm comfort.

Susan congratulated herself again on wearing slacks and flat shoes. However, as she took a step over the scrubbed deck, her leather soles slipped. Danny did not embarrass her by reacting; he just supported her.

"Well, Lord love us! You've brought a lady friend. Well, Danny boy, are you gonna introduce me?"

"Rummy Smith, meet Susan Stead."

Susan grinned at the old man. He was short, stocky, with a mass of brilliant white hair shooting straight up from his low forehead, and a rosy, bulbous nose. She acknowledged the introduction. "Mr. Smith."

"Aw, call me Rummy. Mr. Smith sounds like an insurance salesman." The worst kind of person, his tone implied.

Susan liked the comfortable interior of the *Jacques II*. It was richly masculine, if a bit tattered and worn. The walls and cabinets were red mahogany. There was a narrow gas stove, an apartment-size refrigerator, a cutting-block countertop, and a white enamel sink. To the left of the sink was a heavy, old-fashioned radio unit.

She wanted to explore through a door deeper along but Rummy waved his thumb toward a narrow, bench-like couch, upholstered in checkered fabric, which circled three sides of a table. Susan slid along until she was at the back.

When Danny sat to her right, she angled her legs away from him. She did not want the warmth of his leg to distract her from the purpose of the visit. Just knowing that Danny was there gave Susan a warm feeling of awareness. She felt alive and, in some unfathomable way, proud to be with him.

Rummy filled a kettle and placed it over the flame. "I suppose you brought some of that perfume you drink?" He sneered at Danny.

"As a matter of fact." Smiling, Danny produced a couple of tea bags with brightly colored paper wrappers and a string attached to each.

"Lord love us, will you look at that." Rummy picked one up with the tip of his thumb and forefinger, like a dead bug, and sniffed it. "You don't drink this stuff, do you?" he asked Susan.

"Anything will be fine," she answered, then remembered Harkey's warning. "Ah, black coffee . . . or tea. A great spot you've got here." She indicated the cabin. "Have you lived aboard long?"

"Going on twenty years," he answered proudly.

"On this boat . . . ship?" She wondered when a boat became a ship.

"Yes, on this boat. I can see you're from the city."

She ignored the last comment. "It's very nice."

"Yep. She's a beauty. Built in the 1930s for rum-running. You ever heard of rum-running, missy?"

"Of course. Were you a rumrunner?"

Danny interjected, "Aw, Susan, don't get him started."

Rummy waved him silent "Yes, I was a runner, and darn good at it too!"

"On this?" Susan looked around.

"You don't need to say it like that! The *Jacques II* is a fine boat."

"Oh no! What I mean is it looks like a big old speed-boat."

Rummy snorted and turned to Danny. "Where'd you find her?" Back to Susan, "Well, of course she's a speed-boat—what do you think rumrunners used? This little beauty had Liberty airplane engines, four hundred and fifty horsepower. Lord love ya, she revved at 2100!"

"But where did you store the liquor?"

Danny slapped the table a couple of times to get their attention. "Don't answer that. We don't have time to hear your stories today, as interesting as they are."

"I'd like to hear them." Susan nodded solemnly. "But he's right. We've got something more important to discuss."

The kettle whistled. Rummy poured water into three mugs while Danny placed coasters around the table.

"What have you heard about our chase on Sunday night?" Danny asked.

Plunking a mug in front of Susan, Rummy answered, "I heard you went after a seiner running without lights and lost 'em."

Danny looked sheepish. "We never had them to lose them."

"They had quite a lead," Susan interjected. "I reported them. You see, these guys were kidnapping a little girl. They took me too when I got in their way but the man who was driving the boat gave me a life jacket and pushed me over the side."

"The skipper," Danny said. "Describe him for us."

Susan thought back. "He looked about thirty. Had a potbelly, but he wasn't fat, more swaybacked. But the interesting thing was that he referred to another man as Dad."

Rummy had squeezed in on Susan's left, his knees splayed under the table. The moment they pushed against hers she shifted. The warmth of Danny's leg seeped through her slacks. She glanced at him.

"Called him Dad?" Rummy pursed his lips and stared at the bulkhead. "Father-and-son combination on a herring seiner."

After a moment Danny said, "Can't be too many of them."

"Bah! There's plenty." Rummy snapped his head back. "Drink your perfume, Shipley. I can't sit around gnawing the fat with you all day."

Susan glanced from one man's face to the other. Danny looked perplexed but Rummy was clearly agitated.

"Well, who are they?" Danny asked. "Come on, Rummy, these guys might still have that kid, and they beat up Susan."

Rummy looked at her cheek. "Naw, the two I had in mind wouldn't hurt nobody."

She hoped the culprits were in fact the men he had in mind, since they "wouldn't hurt nobody."

Danny tried again. "Well, who are they?"

"I ain't smearing nobody's good name without first

checking facts. Must be hundreds of fathers and sons working this shore. Drink up your tea now."

Susan said, "We won't do anything unless we're pretty sure. I could go and see these guys and if I recognize them, then we'll call the RCMP."

"Say," Rummy demanded, "how come the Mounties haven't been to see me yet?" Clearly his pride was hurt.

Susan answered, "They don't believe me, because Amy's parents say that she's not missing."

"Who're the parents?"

"Robert and Deidra Sutherland. Know them?"

Rummy shook his head. "Naw."

"Well, what do you say?" Danny reminded. "Are you going to tell us who you suspect so Susan and I can check them out?"

"No, I'm not. I'm no informant. You two run along now so I can get some work done around here." He slid off the bench and opened a door below the sink, emerging a moment later to hand Danny a bulging grocery bag knotted at the top. "Take this along with you."

"He wants us to put out his garbage," Danny explained, hooking his index finger through the loop. As they prepared to leave he pressed, "You'll let us know, eh? Call us as soon as you hear anything?"

"I'll let you know if I hear anything. Probably won't. Even if I did it wouldn't be for a while, mind. Fishermen work for a living, not like some people I know." He raised an eyebrow at Danny.

"When do you think you'll be able to see them?" Susan asked.

They emerged on the deck and Rummy peered at the overcast sky. "If it stays calm they likely won't be back into port till after sunset."

"Should we come back then?"

"Naw, I know where Danny boy lives." He winked at Susan. "I'll see you two there, if there's something I figure needs saying."

Chapter Ten

Susan and Danny jumped off the boat and trudged up the wharf to a rusty oil drum chained to a hefty rock. When Danny yanked off the wooden lid a pungent stink mingled with the damp fog air.

"Does he do that often?" Susan pointed to the bag in his hand. "Give his guests his garbage?"

"Yup." He stuffed the bag inside and replaced the lid. "Hates to have anything cluttering up his boat."

"I suppose it stands to reason, living in a small space like that."

"Yep, yep." He did not immediately turn toward the Coast Guard station but scratched the back of his neck, then jammed his hands in his pockets. The ocean breeze ruffled his hair so that blond bangs flopped down over his eyes.

"You haven't had much luck finishing your drinks this morning, not much luck at all."

"That's right," Susan said, remembering the un-touched tea on Rummy's table.

He nodded toward a rocky drive heading inland. "Come on, let's go up to the Seal Harbor. It's just up a ways."

He leaned forward as if waiting on her answer was the most important thing he had to do. Susan assumed that it was another one of his mannerisms, but she felt flattered all the same.

"Yes, yes. Let's."

A crop of boulders, still slimy from the moisture in the air, slipped under Susan's leather soles. Danny crooked an elbow and she hooked her arm into his. His forearm felt rock-hard under her fingers. Her eyes fol-lowed the line of his arm to his chest where the soft fabric of his shirt draped over rounded muscles. She glanced up to find Danny considering her with a crooked smile.

"Rummy thinks you'll be at my place tonight," he said.

Heat flooded her face. "He jumped to conclusions, I'd say."

"Just a little premature, perhaps?"

She wasn't sure how to respond to his flirting. He was a handsome guy, but she felt all coiled up with tension. She was glad he was with her, though. Despite his height, he felt solid, compact, and she needed someone to lean on at that moment.

She returned to the conversation on the boat. "Who-ever they are—the people who matched my description—they must be friends of his."

Danny sobered. "Likely, likely they are. Rummy's been around since I was a kid, living on a pension, I guess. Spends a lot of time drinking with the local fishermen, playing cards on his boat or up at the social club. He knows everybody."

"Will he be all right? I mean, these guys are dangerous. He'll watch out, won't he?"

"As well as anyone could, I guess. Despite his age, Rummy's tough. Spends a lot of time reliving his past. Rumrunners got used to taking risks, keeping secrets, and dodging people. He's proud of that."

They walked along the twisty road toward the restaurant. Whenever a car approached they squeezed close together on the narrow gravel shoulder to let it pass. One tooted the horn and Danny raised the flat of his hand toward them in greeting, but he didn't loosen the grip on her arm.

"You'll call me as soon as you hear from him, won't you?"

"Sure."

"Don't let me forget to give you my phone number."

Danny snickered. "Not to worry, I won't."

He was flirting again. Susan rolled her face away from him to hide her confusion. How could she be feeling pleased at a time like this?

Danny held the door of the Seal Harbor Restaurant and Social Club wide and guided her through. Inside the air reeked of fried foods and stale smoke. The frizzy-haired waitress behind the take-out counter smiled blandly at Susan but grinned freely the moment she saw Danny.

"Well, hello stranger, haven't seen you in a dog's age. Where have you been keeping yourself?"

" 'Morning, Nora," he said. "Meet my friend Susan."

"Hi, Susan," Nora said warmly and studied her face. "You've been in here before."

"Sure, I drop in once in a while."

Danny added, "Her great-aunt lives over at the retirement home."

"Oh yeah, what's her name?"

Susan said, "Polly . . . Pauline Gray."

As Susan waited, ignored, the waitress and Danny speculated about her aunt. Who was her family tree? Where had she lived? Wasn't she friends with so-and-so? Susan didn't feel insulted. This was the kind of conversation she'd come to expect whenever she met someone new in Seal Harbor. Eventually Danny and Nora passed a favorable judgment on her Aunt Polly's character. Susan smiled, oddly pleased that they linked her with the community. When she analyzed her own reaction, she assumed that the link added a certain weight to her right to search for Amy. It made it almost normal that she and Danny Shipley should work together. Until Amy was found, she was going to work with him and with anyone else who could conceivably help her find that child.

"So, what can I get for you?" Nora asked.

"I'd like a coffee, black please," Susan said quickly.

When Danny ordered peach juice the waitress smiled indulgently at Susan. "He's got us well trained, eh? We keep all his fancy juices and them heavy breads out back."

After they settled at a table, Danny smoothed his moustache a moment, then said, "Okay. What I've been wondering, what I can't figure out is—oh, here's our order. Thanks, Nora."

When the waitress had left them alone again he said, "What's the motive? If they took Amy for ransom you'd think that she'd be home by now, with Sutherland poorer, but Amy safe at home."

"Remember I told you about CNR's assets, offshore exploration rights and the like? How they're being dispersed? It occurred to me that the kidnappers could be waiting until CORE. Remember they said that awful thing about keeping her, ah, alive until next week? Well, CORE is on this weekend."

He sipped his thick juice then licked the moustache on his upper lip. "Core?"

"Canadian Offshore Resources Exhibition. It's a huge display of everything and everybody that has anything to do with offshore oil. Sutherland is going to announce the successful bidders during the last day."

"So you think someone's going to exchange his daughter for the offshore rights?"

"His stepdaughter," Susan corrected. "Amy is his step-daughter. I don't know if that makes any difference, but he referred to her as such, so I wondered."

"Hmm, I don't know. What do you think the offshore rights are worth?"

"Millions." Susan had a thought. "But there's the po-litical side to it too. They're Canadian resources. What if some foreign power wanted to gain control over the world's oil—control prices somehow? What if Suther-land found out?"

"And they're holding his kid to keep him quiet? Boy, if that's the case, this is more serious than ever. I mean, the ramifications."

"Maybe I'd better call the RCMP and tell them."

Danny shook his head slowly. "I doubt they'd listen to you. Remember, they don't think a crime has been committed."

Susan nodded. "Other than the assault on me."

"And they're not going to spend much time on that," Danny said ruefully. "Not much time at all."

"Well, I guess I better get myself assigned to CORE on Friday. See what I can find out. I'll talk to everybody who shows any interest in CNR or Robert Sutherland."

"Assigned?"

"The company I work for, Sampson Corp., has a booth

there. I'll work it, demonstrate equipment, pass out brochures, that sort of thing."

"You work for Sampson? The international corporation?"

"Yes. Didn't I tell you? I sell office equipment for them. I can sign up to work our booth."

Danny looked pensive. "Well, I guess you'd be safe enough at an exhibition, around all those people."

"I do it all the time; it's my job." With that thought she glanced at her watch and grimaced.

Danny said, "You know what I mean. The way you described him, Amy's father doesn't sound normal."

"The worst he can do is yell at me, and I've lived through that before."

Chapter Eleven

The next morning Susan arrived at Sampson Corporation desperately anxious to hear news of Amy so, without really being conscious of her actions, she reached for the phone book to look up the number of the Seal Harbor Coast Guard Station. Her hand arrested in midair.

The busy bullpen was no place to make that type of call. She needed to be alone to compose her thoughts before talking to Danny Shipley. Besides, Gordon Moore was lurking somewhere nearby and, if he caught her making a private call, he would enjoy the excuse to reprimand her. So she phoned Mary MacDonald, Robert Sutherland's assistant, instead.

"Hello, Mary," she recited the lines she had decided upon in bed that morning. "This is Susan Stead, remember, the Sampson rep?" Mary did—how could she not? "I was wondering if we could have lunch today, on Sampson's tab, of course?" The extra moment it took Mary to answer caused Susan some anxiety.

"Well, okay," Mary said. "Where do you want to meet?"

Meet? Of course, Susan thought, she didn't want The Boss to see them together. "How about the Clipper?"

"That sounds nice. I don't usually break for lunch until one."

"Great! I'll see you then."

She hung up and rubbed her hands together. Now she'd get the scoop about Robert Sutherland.

She flipped open the business directory to the list of companies who dealt with the offshore oil industry. Even though she only jotted down those who were in the heart of the city, her territory, the list was extensive—owners of supply ships, temporary personnel companies, geologists, machinists—dozens of services. There had to be some industry gossip about CNR, and she meant to hear it all.

Still, the morning dragged by. She visited a dozen companies who let her go through their supply closets and fill out an order form according to what she found there. While they signed the order she asked questions. How did they feel about the CNR dissolution? Did they have dealings with them in the past? Who did they think would get the exploration rights?

The investigation turned up very little she had not already read in the newspapers. A number of newcomers to Halifax were devoting a lot of time and money in their bid to replace CNR. They came from all over: Alberta, the North Sea, Texas, Germany, and a number of Arab investors. Susan resolved to pay calls on them after her lunch with Mary MacDonald.

She arrived at the Clipper Restaurant a few minutes early. Three walls of the upper level of the restaurant were glass with small round tables crowded before them. As usual, the place was packed. Although the food was no better than dozens of other restaurants around the city, it had a prestigious reputation and did a thriving business. Today there was a bite to the damp salt air so she aimed at an interior table overlooking the Halifax harbor front.

"Gosh, I hope I'm not late," Mary gushed as she slid into the empty chair. The plaid pattern in the knit material of her dress shrunk to tidy dark squares around her waist but stretched large and pale over her hips and bust.

Susan caught the eye of the bar waiter. "Would you like something while we look over the menu? Perhaps a glass of wine?"

"Umm . . ." Mary hesitated. "Oh, why not."

Susan ordered a wine for Mary and a soda for herself. Except for a few innocuous comments about the weather, the two women sipped their drinks in silence and perused the menu. By the time the waiter placed their meals before them and wished them a curt "*bon appétit*," Susan had worked her courage up to speak.

She prodded at her quiche. "I expect you're wondering why I asked you to lunch. One reason is that I wanted to apologize for the scene I caused yesterday."

Mary's fork hovered in midair. "No need. I understand."

"Do you? Did Mr. Sutherland tell you what I said?"

"No. He went out right after you and didn't come back until this morning."

Susan digested this bit of news. Perhaps he couldn't stand to sit around his office without doing something, anything, to get Amy back. On the other hand, he might have been arranging for the two thugs to intimidate her in the coffee shop.

"I'd like to tell you the whole story, Mary. You see, you might be able to throw some light on it, to explain Sutherland, or something. On the other hand, I have to ask you to treat what I'm about to tell you in complete confidentiality. Do you agree?"

"If you don't want me to talk about whatever this is, I won't." Mary rested her fork on the edge of her plate of Digby scallops and looked attentive.

Susan gave her a tight-lipped smile. "Late Sunday night I went to Crescent Beach. Two men came up the beach and they had Amy Sutherland. You know, carrying her. She was fighting them, you understand. They were kidnapping her!"

For a moment Mary's mouth gaped open, then she lifted the white linen napkin and dabbed at her lips, then at her nose. She seemed to be focused at a spot about halfway across the table, facing Susan but not seeing her.

"Well, like an idiot"—Susan almost spit out the word—"I walked right up to them and asked what was going on. I was so stupid, but by the time I realized . . . they had us."

Mary raised her eyes. "They did that to you?"

Susan nodded and fingered the bruise on her face. "Yeah. Anyway, to make a long story short, I got away but they still had Amy on a fishing boat headed out to sea. The RCMP are telling me to forget the whole incident, but how can I? So yesterday I went to see Sutherland to ask him how I could help, but, well, you heard him—he blew up."

"What did he say about all this?" Mary asked.

"He denied it. Said he had breakfast with Amy yesterday morning and she was fine."

"But you don't believe him?"

"I don't know what to believe. That's why I wanted to speak to you. Has he been acting differently lately? Do you think he's worried?"

"Of course he's acting differently. We're being closed down. Canadian Natural Resources was his baby. Of course he's been upset. But whether or not his stepdaughter's missing, well, frankly, he wasn't any different yesterday than he's been for weeks."

"What about his reaction to me?"

"As I say, he's under tremendous pressure these days."

"But you said he went out and didn't come back."

"He doesn't always tell me where he's going, these days especially. Most of the staff has already been laid off. There's nothing much more for him to do except grant the CNR licenses to private industry. He's probably even decided that already—had all the offers for weeks."

Susan stared out the window. The squat Halifax–Dartmouth Ferry glided slowly by. "I guess what I'm asking is . . ." She turned a concerned face to Mary. "Do you think that Amy Sutherland is safe at home? Is he acting like a man whose daughter is safe at home?"

Mary answered quickly, "Frankly, yes."

"Do you know him personally? Have you been to his house? Met his wife?"

"Sure, I've arranged parties out there. It was a convenient place to hold them, a good setup. Robert signed some significant deals at his house parties."

"Do you know Amy?"

"Yes. She's a cute little kid."

"You can understand why I'm so worried about her then."

Mary speared a scallop. "I don't think you should worry. If Robert said that Amy was safe at home, she is. Please understand, I don't doubt your story, but couldn't it have been another child you saw? Perhaps her daddy was dragging her around because the child was throwing a temper tantrum."

Susan didn't know what to think. "I want to believe that, of course I do. But it was Amy Sutherland I saw on that beach."

"What are you planning to do about it? What are you going to do next?"

"Boy, I don't know." Susan held the palms of her hands in the air and shrugged. "Maybe I should drop it."

Mary smiled. "That would be my advice."

As she nibbled a piece of crisp lettuce, Susan brooded. Could she set aside the incident and get back to her life? She glanced at Mary and saw that she wore a little self-satisfied smile as she sipped her wine.

"What are your plans, Mary, when CNR closes?"

"Oh, I'll go back to Cape Breton." She looked off with a dreamy expression. "I have a boyfriend waiting there."

"Well, good for you." Susan hoped the surprise was not evident in her voice. Why shouldn't she have a boyfriend?

"Are you married? Or, do you have anyone?" Mary asked.

"No." Susan didn't feel like elaborating. "No, I don't."

Once again, Danny Shipley popped into her mind. He definitely would not fit in at the Clipper Restaurant. On the other hand, Susan reminded herself, there was a lot more to that man than showed on the surface. A lot more.

Anxious to hear news of Rummy's inquiry, Susan checked for messages the rest of that day but, by 5:30 when she had returned to the office after making sales calls, Danny still had not called.

The bullpen bustled with Lew, Chuck, and the other sales reps restocking their briefcases with brochures, writing up orders and delivery slips, and commiserating with each other about the day.

As Susan passed Gordon Moore, he looked down his nose at her. "Dressed rather casually, aren't we?"

According to the unwritten Sampson dress code, women did not wear trousers and flat shoes to work. Susan blatantly compared her neat pantsuit with his wrinkled, pin-striped suit and jibed, "Oh, I wouldn't worry about it too much, Gordon. Not too many customers see you now that you're driving a desk."

Lew and Chuck, eavesdropping nearby, guffawed. A muscle in Moore's jaw twitched where he gritted his teeth together.

"By the way," Susan spoke clearly, "I want to go on the list to man the booth at CORE."

He was immediately suspicious. "Why?"

"Why not? Maybe it's because you recommended it a few weeks ago and I'm taking your advice."

"That'd be a first."

"So, who do I see about the booth schedule?"

Moore shrugged. "My secretary. She's left for the day. Leave a note on her desk." He walked off.

Susan strolled over to Lew and Chuck but before she had a chance to say anything the outside line buzzed and she was paged to the phone.

She snatched one nearby and pushed the line. "Susan Stead."

"Hi Susan, it's Danny Shipley." His voice sounded calm and slow. Susan covered one ear to block the frenzied atmosphere of the bullpen.

"Did you hear from Rummy?"

"Yes, but he only said that the word around the docks is that the guys he wanted to see—he wouldn't say suspected—must be swordfishing. Haven't been around in almost a week."

"Is that normal?"

"Oh sure, depending on where they went."

"I forgot to mention to Rummy the partitions that I tripped on that night. He could check if the boat he's considering has them."

"They do. I asked him. He admitted that it's a purse seiner, all right, but he still won't identify it."

"Is there anyone else we can ask? Department of Fisheries?"

"I'll think on it. I'm going over to the social club tonight. I'll ask around about who has a seiner out for swordfish, check the father/son angle."

"Oh, that'd be great."

"No, don't get your hopes up. These guys could live down Digby way or up in Cape Breton and Rummy would still know them. He's like that. No reason to expect they'd be from around these parts. But I'll let you know if I learn anything."

Susan felt a tinge of disappointment. All afternoon she toyed with the idea of going to Danny's home to await Rummy's call and now he wasn't even going to be home.

"Well, have fun," she said, hoping he would ask her to join him.

"Will do," he answered briefly. " 'Bye."

Deflated, Susan hung up the phone and wove her way between the desks and chairs to her own cramped space. She took out her calendar and tried to think of companies who would need new office equipment, but her heart wasn't in it. She could go home to her empty condo and another night of worrying about Amy. Instead she reached for the phone book and looked up the Seal Harbor Coast Guard Station's number. After the phone rang a few times she remembered, except for being on call, they knocked off at 4:00. She searched through the book again and found Shipley, D. Danny answered on the first ring.

"Hi, Danny, it's Susan."

"Well, hello again!" He sounded pleased.

"You haven't left yet."

"We're just getting ready to head out now."

We are? That wiped the smile off her face. He was already with someone. Now she didn't feel she could very well ask if she could go along that night. She hoped that there wasn't a woman listening to his side of the conversation, someone who would wonder just who this woman was who was calling him. On the other hand, nothing ventured, nothing gained.

"So, what's up?" he asked.

Susan said in a rush, "The reason I called is that I wondered if you would like to get together to talk about things we can do to get Amy back? Maybe we could go out to supper or something?"

"Sure!" he said. "I haven't had a night in town in months. Are you free tomorrow night?"

"Yes, say about seven-thirty?"

"Seven-thirty Thursday night. It's a date."

A date? Well, she supposed she had just asked him out on a date. After giving him directions to her building, Susan said, "You be careful the bad guys don't get you tonight." She pictured the two hoods in the coffee shop and frowned.

"Hey," he answered, "not to worry. I'm gonna sit with my back to the wall."

Chapter Twelve

Thursday morning Susan swung her briefcase to the front of her legs and squeezed both hands around its cushioned leather handle. She told herself not to be nervous. She had every right to visit CNR. After all, they were the biggest sponsor of CORE and would know a great deal about the event. It would be natural that, the day before the show was to be set up, a booth attendant like herself would call upon them for information. Perfectly natural.

She desperately wanted to avoid Robert Sutherland so she stepped gingerly into the reception area and asked, "Is Mary MacDonald at her desk? I have a couple of questions about CORE."

The woman removed her blue-rimmed glasses. "Yes, she is. Do you want me to announce you?"

"No, thanks. I know the way."

She slowed her step at the end of the hallway and peeked around the corner. Sutherland's office door was closed and Mary, digging in a file drawer, had her back to Susan.

"Hi," Susan said softly.

Startled, Mary leapt away from the cabinet and froze, knees flexed. For a long second she stared wild-eyed at Susan, then she darted a look at the file drawer and slammed it shut.

"Gosh, I'm sorry." Susan gulped. "I didn't mean to frighten you."

Color flooded Mary's face and she tittered. "Oh, no, that's all right."

"I got assigned to the Sampson booth for the trade show. If you're not too busy, could you go over the floor plan with me?" Susan rambled nervously. "I always get turned around at trade shows, especially something the size of CORE—well, you don't get any bigger than that. I'm sure it'll be day three before I even find our spot."

"I see. No problem," Mary said, shooting a look toward Sutherland's door. "I've got the plan tacked up in the supply room."

"Could I see it? I'd be really grateful."

Mary led her to an unmarked door to the left of Sutherland's and into a long, narrow room with a window on the end. Floor-to-ceiling metal shelves, stacked with boxes, lined the left side, but on the right wall, the one bordering Sutherland's office, was a massive sheet of paper.

"This is beautifully done," Susan said, admiring the neatly labeled rows of squares. She set her briefcase on the floor.

"It's the master we used for the printers." Mary looked at it proudly. "I finished it a week ago. There's bound to be some changes, but it's basically correct." She leaned closer to the wall and read, "Sampson—Building B, Booth 127–131. Your company has booked a large space. Here it is."

Susan memorized a path from the main door to the booth location. "This is great. Thanks. By the way, I hear CNR is throwing a big reception. Is it open to anyone?"

Mary's face grew animated. "We're giving out invitations at our booth—first come, first served."

Susan asked brazenly, "Could I take a couple now? Two."

"I . . . um, I don't see why not." Mary scurried back to her desk, yanked open a drawer, and thumbed two cardboard slips off the top of the box of invitations.

"Thank you," had barely crossed Susan's lips when the door behind her flew open.

"Mary, have you had—" Sutherland stopped the moment he spied Susan. "What are you doing here?"

Susan looked pleadingly at Mary for help but could not catch her eye. "I . . ." She faltered then, growing angry at his rudeness. "I came to find out about the Sampson Booth at CORE."

"I don't want you around here."

"Oh, for heaven's sake . . ."

"I mean it." He swung on Mary. "Call security if she doesn't leave immediately."

Susan ground out the words. "Where do you get off treating me like I'm the bad guy! You've got a nerve, buddy, when all I wanted to do was help Amy."

"There's nothing wrong with Amy, I told you."

"Then where is she? Just answer that. I was at your house yesterday and she was nowhere to be seen."

"Butt out! I'm warning you! Butt out!"

Susan faced him squarely and hissed, "Listen to me. Just listen to me. I do not want that child hurt. I swear, if—"

"Do you think I do!" he bellowed. "Do you think I do?"

Susan's voice rose to a squeak. "I don't know. You

don't seem at all interested in what I might be able to tell you."

"There is nothing—let me repeat—there is *nothing* you can tell me." He leaned toward her and hissed, "Your snooping around can only cause trouble."

She whispered back, "Are you saying that I might be jeopardizing something? Are you saying you have it all under control?"

"I'm not saying anything other than get out."

"This is a Crown Corporation, and I'm a taxpayer. I have a right to be here."

He swung on his heel, stomped into his office, and slammed the door.

Susan first glanced at Mary, who stared open-mouthed toward Sutherland's office, then down to the reception tickets crushed in her hand. She unfolded them with shaking fingers.

Susan's briefcase was still in the supply room. As soon as she stepped inside, an overwhelming doubt descended. Sutherland was so sure, so emphatic, so desperate. Perhaps she was jeopardizing Amy's safe return. Perhaps he knew exactly what he had to do and did not want her interfering and ruining his plans. Why then did he refuse to talk with her? If she only knew that he had a plan, she would quit poking her nose into it.

She leaned her forehead on the cool drywall. Suddenly she stiffened, held her breath, and then turned her head so her ear flattened to the wall.

Robert Sutherland's voice was muffled, but to Susan the words tolled clearly. "Operator, connect me to the ship-to-shore operator. Yes! The marine operator."

At a sharp sound behind her Susan snapped to attention.

Mary stood at the door. "I think you better go now."

"Oh, Mary!" she whispered. "He's calling the marine operator. You know what that could mean?"

"You better leave." Mary's eyes glared cold and hard.

"But wait! Wait! I've found out a few things. There's this father and son in Seal Harbor who might be involved."

Mary put her hands over her ears and shook her head back and forth. "Stop."

"Mary, listen, I'm working with a man from the Coast Guard. As soon as I see the faces of the guys, I'll know them. Maybe that's why Sutherland doesn't want me around."

Mary looked appalled. "I'm calling security." She backed away, fled to her desk, and began dialing.

Susan picked up her briefcase and slunk out of the office.

That evening, as she moved around her apartment preparing for her date with Danny, Susan relived the encounter in the CNR supply room and groaned. How embarrassing. And yet, she may have learned something important. It could be that Sutherland was in contact with the kidnappers. On the other hand, she reminded herself, he had every right to call the marine operator. He was probably contacting a supply vessel about a CNR matter.

Damp from her bath and wrapped in a terry housecoat, she slid open her closet door and eyed the long row of clothes: business suits and dresses, a few good woollen trousers with coordinated silk blouses. Danny Shipley was so casual. What could she wear that wouldn't look out of place beside him? Susan had never seen him when he wasn't on Coast Guard duty. What did she really know about him?

He wasn't pretentious. He preferred natural foods so he probably liked natural fabrics. Susan burrowed deep into her closet for her cotton midcalf-length skirt and a matching blouse. Someone once told her that the deep gold and maroon colors set off the red highlights in her hair.

She dug the outfit out and threw it on the chair beside the cupboard that hid the ironing board. After pressing her outfit, Susan twisted her hair into a coil and secured it with a macramé clip that her sister had made for her many years ago. She thought that Danny would approve.

Dressed and ready to go, she hovered at the door and surveyed her apartment. Smooth lines, pale colors, modern and tidy. He would hate it. She was still frowning when the intercom buzzed so her voice snapped abruptly as she thumbed down the button, "Yes?"

"Susan? It's Danny." His voice echoed in the tinny speaker.

Susan said, "Come on up," as she held the security door button. A moment later he sauntered down the long hall toward her.

"Well, you found it," she said inanely.

She watched his face as he entered her home. For an instant he looked like he had a bad taste in his mouth, then he glanced at her and smiled. "You give good directions."

He stepped a couple of paces over the thick dove-gray carpet, backed up, and heeled off his mud-covered shoes. Susan did not stop him.

Danny patted at the rear of his jeans as though dust would billow off them. "Lord, I don't know what to do in a place like this. White furniture—what next!"

As she debated about whether or not she should be offended, Susan caught sight of Danny's eyes. They twinkled.

"Would you like a cup of tea? A glass of wine?"

"Tea would be great. Any kind. Thanks."

She started for the kitchen. "How did it go last night?"

"I think I've got a lead."

She started to fill the kettle, but his words had her hurrying back out into the living room. "Oh yeah?"

"There's this guy, Sammy Spinney. Apparently he's been living out west for a couple of years. Just got back. His dad's purse seiner hasn't been at its berth for a week or so." He raised an eyebrow and looked sidelong at Susan.

"What does he look like?"

"About thirty, beer gut. Spinney's boat is turquoise, with the tender secured to the top of the cabin." He looked at her questioningly.

"Hmm. It's possible, but I couldn't really tell the color, not in the dark." She fetched two cups with matching saucers and carefully put them on her coffee table. "A father-and-son team? You called them the Spinneys?"

"That's right. I tried to check them out today. Seems his mother is around. My mom saw her at the grocery store. She said that her old man was swordfishing."

"That's what Rummy said." The palm of her hands dampened. "Why would they take Amy? What's the motive?"

"Money. The price of herring's at an all-time low. Bank's calling in their note. But hey, we don't know it's them."

Susan paced in front of the window. "What should we do? Should we tell the RCMP?"

Danny shook his head. "I'd hate to heap more trouble on the Spinneys if they didn't do it. They're well liked in Seal Harbor. People have a lot of sympathy for them. I mean, it could happen to any fisherman. A run of bad luck."

"I hardly think that most fishermen would resort to crime because of a run of bad luck!"

"All the more reason to hold off on accusing them without proof."

"Well, we've got to do something." Susan couldn't keep still.

"I've been thinking about that, trying to come up with a reason I can get the fleet to keep an eye open for the Spinney boat."

"Oh, Danny." Susan moaned. "There's not much time. CORE starts tomorrow and you know what they said." Her heart sank. Poor Amy. Suddenly she felt weak and close to tears.

Danny jumped to his feet and put his hands on her shoulders. "Hey, this is good news. If these two have Amy, she's safe. These aren't some terrorists out to capture the world oil supply. They're a couple of fishermen down on their luck."

Susan fingered her faded bruise. "If it is them, they're not alone."

Danny's solemn face was inches from her. She noticed little things: the tip of his nose was sunburned and tender looking; his eyelashes were very long, red at the base and transparent on their curled ends. His eyes looked like crystal, lit from within. The heat rose to her face, and her mind raced, confused. She'd never had such conflicting feelings as these before. On one hand she was worried and anxious and guilty. On the other hand she felt attracted to Danny.

"What do you want to do?" he asked quietly. "Do you want to call the Mounties?"

"They won't go looking for a kid who's not even missing."

He stared silently for a moment. "There's nothing we can do right now." He asked in a husky whisper, "Why don't we try to forget it for tonight?"

He was right. There wasn't anything she could do for Amy at that moment. She wasn't a bad person because she wanted to slide into Danny's arms. Desperately needing to be comforted, she laid her head on the crook of his shoulder. He gathered her close. For a moment, they stood like that, just hugging. She could hear his heart thudding.

"We could order a pizza or something, if you don't feel up to going out," he said a moment later.

She stepped back and cleared her throat. It felt as if his eyes were looking right into her heart, but she wasn't embarrassed because he obviously felt just as attracted to her as she did to him. "No, I'd like to go out."

The elevator arrived after a brief wait, and they stood with their faces tilted up at the numbers. As they crossed the modern foyer of her building Susan watched their reflections in the vast window. Danny walked with a spring to his step, his feet slightly splayed. When he guided her through the doors and onto the sidewalk he kept his hand pressed to her lower back. The moist evening air tingled on her skin.

Outside a taxi smoothed to a stop along the building's semicircle driveway and a couple emerged, smiling. Susan was looking toward them when she asked, "Where are you park—" Her voice arrested at the expression on the faces of the two strangers—mouths agape, fear! As she jerked her head to follow their look she was thrown off her feet.

A sharp crack! A tremendous crash. Oomph! Danny landed on top of her.

He pulled her up and yanked on her arm. Stumbling, they crossed the few yards toward a long cement planter. A woman screamed. Susan craned her neck and saw it— a car reversing. A rifle barrel pointed toward her!

She fell hard on her stomach on the grass and wiggled beside Danny into the dark shadow of the planter. His hand searched around the ground and came back with a large stone. Susan scraped up a handful of gravel, tearing her skin, and threw it wildly over the planter in the direction of the car. Tires screeched and a car accelerated away. Frantic voices bubbled. The car had gone.

Danny's head was silhouetted against the foyer windows as he peeked over the top of the planter. He twisted and sagged against the cement with his legs stretched across the grass. Susan scrambled closer and ran her hands over his chest and shoulders searching for damage.

"Danny, are you okay? Danny?" He seemed unhurt.

"I'm fine. How about you? Did anything hit you?" Danny smoothed the hair on the back of her head.

"I don't think so." Her elbow throbbed. "What happened?"

"I saw the barrel and I didn't even think," he said. "I just pushed you down." His body tensed and he raised her face to the light. "You're sure you're okay?"

People spilled out of the building. A plate-glass window lay shattered, light glinting off the fragments. The woman from the taxi approached, stepping gingerly over the glass, her hands held in little fists at her chest. Leaning toward Susan, she gasped. "Who are you? Why were they trying to kill you?"

Chapter Thirteen

"**I** know someone tried to kill you," DeLong bellowed, marching from behind the heavy wooden table. "What you're hiding from me is why. Why you? Why now?"

Susan rolled her head back on her shoulders and sighed. Danny, who massaged her tense muscles, tried not to interrupt. They were in an interview room somewhere in the interior of the RCMP building, had been there for a couple of tense, unpleasant hours.

Susan sighed dejectedly. "I've told you over and over again. They know I saw their faces. They probably want to silence me. I might recognize the men who stole Amy."

"Why did they wait until now? They could have killed you days ago."

She sounded exasperated. "I don't know. They must have found out who I am. That I've been asking questions."

"To whom?"

Danny held up a hand. "Wait a minute now. We're just going around in circles."

DeLong turned on him. "And we will keep going around in circles until I get some answers." He fixed his gaze on Susan. "Who did you talk to?"

"Um, Amy's father, no one else."

"You didn't tell anyone else about this kidnapping theory?" he asked cynically.

"Yes, I told you. I told my friend Marty, and Danny here, and Sutherland's assistant."

"And Rummy Smith," Danny added. "He's a friend of mine who lives in Seal Harbor. But you know all this. Come on, DeLong. Susan's all done in. Let's call it a night."

DeLong glared at Susan. "Not until I get some answers."

Susan stood. "I've told you everything I know! Told you and told you."

Danny wrapped an arm about her shoulders and led her toward the door as he spoke over his shoulder, "I'm going to take Susan to my place tonight if you think of any new questions. Why don't you get out there and find the guys who shot at her, eh?"

"I'm not finished yet," DeLong barked.

Susan rounded on him. "And I'm not under arrest, so you can't hold me."

They headed down an antiseptic hallway with Mark DeLong close on their heels. "I still say you're trying to hide something from me and I promise you I'll find out what it is."

Susan snapped, "I am not. If I could think of anything that would help I'd tell you. Don't you think I want Amy found?"

"Why did you refuse to let the officer at the cottage take you to a hospital that night?"

"What?"

"You heard me. Why did you immediately have a bath? Why didn't you do the sensible thing and let the experts take a look at what you had under your fingernails? After all, you said you fought off the attackers."

"I never thought . . . I suppose I should have." Her shoulders slumped forward and her face sagged in remorse.

"And why were you there on that beach that night?"

"I told you, I like it there. I've done it dozens of times. Haven't you gone to the beach to watch the waves?"

"Not in the middle of the night."

"It wasn't the middle of the night!" She stepped out the door.

Danny clasped her shoulder and guided her toward his truck. When he pulled out of the parking lot, DeLong was still standing on the top of the brick steps with his hands on his hips.

They made the drive to Seal Harbor almost in silence. The hours with the Halifax Police, then the inquisition with the Mounties, left them both drained. Danny knew it was worse for Susan. Now she huddled with her legs and arms tightly crossed.

"Don't take it personally. I've seen them grill witnesses lots of times; they're always like that."

"Hmm?" Susan barely moved her head.

"They don't have any sympathy, for one thing. Well, that's not right. But, the way they treated you like you had something to hide . . . they do that so people keep talking, trying to get the cops to lighten up, you know. People will say anything to get cops to relax. I imagine it gets a lot of results, makes people say things they wouldn't otherwise mention."

He took his eyes off the road to see if she was listening. Susan looked at him and gave a tight little smile. A passing car illuminated her eyes that brimmed with tears.

"Aw, Sus," he softened. "It's okay. You're safe with me. They don't know anything about my place."

"I'm sorry to be so much trouble," she said thickly.

"Don't be silly. I couldn't let you stay on your own on a night like this."

Danny remembered how, a few short hours ago, he had held her tense body until the police siren wailed to a stop a few yards from where they cowered. What he would do if he ever got his hands on the guys that did it! Wanting to punch something, he wrapped his fingers more tightly around the steering wheel.

He looked at her again, but she had turned to face away from him, toward the dim rocks, wind-blown pines, and hills of rough scrub. She wasn't looking at the scenery; it was too dark for that. Besides, the real scenery, the ocean, was on their left. She obviously didn't want to talk so Danny drove silently until he could see, on the distant point, the dim light above his door.

"That's my house, up there," he said, slowing the car to turn in the gravel drive. "This is where my folks live. I guess it's not so late after all. They're still up."

The blue from the television flickered through the window. They rolled past the square house with its white verandah, and past the turnoff to the Shipley wharf. The light at its end made the weathered planks look silver.

A few seconds later, after pulling to a stop beside the side door of his house, Danny shut off the car engine and listened to the waves crashing on the steep rocky shores all around.

"Listen, would you rather stay at my folks' house? They won't mind." He smiled. "Mom loves to have something to tease me about."

"I'm already being too much trouble. I'll just use your sofa, if that's okay."

"Go on in then. I'll get some firewood."

It was only early September, but his house teetered on

the ocean's edge where the brisk air tingled. Rarely a day went by without any fog. Most mornings it blanketed the offshore islands, drifted out to the ocean after a couple of hours of sunlight, then wafted back to shore after supper. Danny loved the fog, the way it softened everything, the way it made the view different and subtle. By September, a fire was a welcome evening comfort.

When he hopped up the couple of stairs with his armload of wood and scuffed across the deck, he that saw Susan waited in a daze a step inside the dark house.

"Flick on that light," he said as he passed her.

The wood crashed into the box. Susan jumped, startled. Danny, pretending he hadn't noticed, opened the potbellied stove with one hand, and reached for the newsprint with the other. It crunched as he balled it. By the time the fire caught the larger chunks of hardwood, Susan was curled up on the end of the sofa with her feet tucked under her and the skirt wrapped about her knees. Her eyes were locked on the closed glass doors of the stove.

He put the kettle on and got a pot of chamomile tea started in a heavy ceramic mug. When it steeped, he handed it to her. "Here, this should help."

"Thanks."

Danny sat and smoothed a strand of hair from her cheek. He searched for a way to comfort her, to bring her out of the daze she had been in since they left Halifax.

"They won't go after you again. There wouldn't be any point. They were probably trying to get to you before you went to the police with what you knew. Instead they forced the police to listen to you. It backfired."

Her hands trembled. She sipped from the tea and put the cup down on the pine end table.

"That's not it," she said very softly.

He leaned closer.

Susan wiped her nose with a tissue and said, "That's not what's bothering me. It's Amy." She turned distressed eyes to him. "If they did this to us, what will . . . did . . . they do to that child?" Her voice thickened. "They're murderers, not fishermen. Murderers!"

A fat tear spilled from her eye and rolled down her cheek. Danny gathered her in his arms and rocked back and forth. "You've done all you could. You've set the cops on them. Shush now."

The cry seemed to do her good because, after a moment, she looked up through damp lashes and asked sheepishly, "Where's your washroom?"

He pointed to a door off the kitchen. "Through there." When she was gone he poked at the fire and thought. Why did they try to kill her? Because she knew their faces? Because she was onto something? If they knew she was investigating, who told them? All these questions had been asked in the cold, impersonal police station but few conclusions were drawn.

"Gee, Danny, I'm sorry to be such trouble." Susan, her face scrubbed clean of both tears and makeup, leaned on the doorframe. She looked younger, beautiful.

He laid aside the poker and rose in a fluid motion. "Will you stop about that."

"Aren't you going to tell me it's a common reaction to shock?" she asked with a timid smile.

Danny thought back to Monday morning and his attempts to ease the tightly-strung woman who sat in his office. It was not only the conversation he remembered, but how her long, stocking-covered legs distracted him. He glanced down. She was barefoot. Without saying anything he slipped into his bedroom for a pair of woolly socks.

Back in the living room he watched as Susan padded about and leaned her face close to each of the prints on the walls: ocean swells, sailing ships, rocky shorelines, each scene surrounded in warm, earth-tone mats and oak frames.

"I like your house."

"You don't need to sound so surprised," he jibed, tossing her the socks.

"It's like a *Country Living Magazine* house, a masculine one." She poked her finger tentatively into a spittoon then asked absentmindedly, "What's this for?"

"Spitting in."

Her hand yanked back and she made a show of wiping it on her skirt. "You do a lot of that, do you?" she joked.

He snickered, relieved that she seemed recovered. How different she was from the spiked-heeled "suit" of his first impression.

His stomach growled. "Put those socks on, there's no carpet in the kitchen. I've got the makings for an omelette."

"Sounds good."

His kitchen was a big square room with large, uncurtained windows and wide pine planks on the floor. The cupboards were a rich oak so, to offset their darkness, Danny had painted the walls white. Noticing that there was dust in the corners of his wide, pine floorboards, he smiled ruefully. His mother would have said it served him right.

Susan was looking around, frowning.

"What's wrong?" Danny asked.

"Don't you even own a coffee machine?"

"Nope. You'll have to settle with Red Rose tea. Fill the kettle, will you? Oh, don't worry. My folks make coffee. We can drop by there in the morning."

"I have to get up really early if I'm going to get back to my place and get dressed in time for the trade show."

Danny pulled his head out of the refrigerator, straightened, and stared at her. "You can't be considering going to that."

"Yes I am. I have to."

He slammed the fridge door. "Why?"

"You know perfectly well why—Sutherland, CNR, all that."

"The police are investigating now, you don't have to."

"Yes I do! They can't go places I can, at least, not without causing suspicion. I'm a Sampson rep; I have a right to be at CORE, to go to the CNR reception. I know the players. I've spent most of the week getting to know everyone who's involved in the offshore and CNR's closing. The police haven't prepared. They won't understand the people involved."

"You'll put yourself in danger again," he said.

The alarm he had immediately felt about her going to CORE subsided. It was true; by posing as their sales representative, she had seen many of the executives who were bidding for the offshore rights.

"What danger? I'll be around thousands of people all the time."

"You've got two tickets to that CNR reception. You'll need a date. I'll go with you. In fact, I'll spend the next three days at CORE."

"As much as I'd like that, it's not practical. You do have a job."

He held up his hand. "End of discussion. I'll call the other skipper now and get him to switch duties." Pointing at the fridge he ordered, "You dig out the omelette fixings."

When he returned from making arrangements with work, he silently observed Susan at his cutting block. Her hair was twisted and hung down the middle of her back. He remembered that when they left her apartment she had her hair up. It was long and loose at the RCMP station. She must have lost the string holder that he had noticed her wearing earlier.

His eyes drifted down to her feet where the knit socks bunched at her ankles. He liked the way she stood, one leg straight and the other bent with the foot curled so she balanced on her toes.

Pretending to inspect the diced mushrooms, he ran his hand up and down her spine. Her skin felt warm through the thin cotton. Was he a cad for thinking about her this way when she was going through such turmoil? Probably.

"Do you have any sliced meat?" she asked.

"Nope. Never eat the stuff."

"Meat?"

"Sliced meat. I eat chicken, fish, the odd bit of red meat."

She made an elaborate show of looking him up and down. "Well, your diet doesn't seem to have done you any harm."

He leered with arched eyebrows.

Susan turned back to her chopping. "You don't smoke, drink caffeine, or eat much meat."

"Don't worry. My mother makes sure I get lots of processed sugar."

With a practiced ease, he deftly tilted the cast-iron fry pan so that the egg ran evenly over the hot surface. Susan stood nearby cutting slices of thick, whole-wheat bread, and laying out the cheddar cheese.

"Boy," Susan said, slapping the flat edge of the knife on the bread. "You could use this bread as a door stop."

"It's good. You'll like it."

She flicked out little hard bits with her fingernail. "What are these?"

"Sunflower seeds."

"Do you eat like this all the time?"

"Next time you come I'll make sure my fridge is better stocked," he said, smiling at her sidelong.

"I can't imagine you doing better than this," Susan said as he handed her a steaming plate.

Danny pretended he was offended. "What do you mean by that? I'll have you know I'm a pretty good cook."

"I didn't mean . . ." Susan started, then she saw he was teasing.

She did not toy with her food like other girls he had had for meals. Her hearty appetite was a good sign, he thought. She was over the physical effects of the attempt on her life.

After they finished eating, Danny dumped the crockery into the sink and dribbled soap over top. His hands were in the hot, sudsy dishwater, so Susan dried. They chatted companionably about how he built the house and his plans to add a solarium. When they returned to the living room the air was warm with the sweet-smelling wood heat. They spent a quiet evening talking and watching the fire. Danny kept a wary eye on Susan. She looked calm and relaxed—happy even. But he reminded himself that she was likely to have further reaction to the shock.

"I'll put some fresh sheets on my bed. You can sleep there; I'll sleep out here."

She patted the arm of the sofa. "Don't be silly. This isn't long enough for you. Besides, I want to watch the fire as I fall asleep. I love watching the flames."

Danny stepped toward the linen closet. His best sheets, the blue ones his mother had given him for Christmas, were buried deep within in the cupboard. He lifted blankets, pillows, and towels across his arms while he searched. Finally he sighted a flash of blue. Susan scooped them from him and started toward the sofa. He flipped on the brass floor lamp, tossed off the cushions, and unfolded the sofa into a double bed.

Once the bed was made up, Danny rushed around getting everything he thought she might need—a new toothbrush, magazines, a glass of water—while Susan changed in the bathroom. The silk pajama top—another gift from his mother—hung almost to her knees.

"Well." Pause. She was so beautiful he felt shaky and tongue-tied and couldn't stop staring at her. "Anything else I can get you?"

"No, it looks very cozy."

"Jump in."

He pulled the blankets under her chin and tucked them snugly around her legs, smoothed a wrinkle on the pillowcase, slid a magazine closer—he could not stop fidgeting.

"Danny." Susan patted the edge of the sofa for him to sit. "I'm fine."

"I know. It's just that you've had quite a shock."

"And you haven't?"

He smiled. "I guess I was there too. It's just that I want to look after you."

"That's sweet." Susan mumbled, "I've got this tremendous nostalgic feeling. The sound of the surf, the smells."

"You like it here?"

"Yes," she said, sounding confused. "It reminds me of all sorts of things. The wood cook stove in my Gran's kitchen, the nights my sister and I tickled each other under the ragged old quilt. We used to hide our little toys in the holes." She snickered ruefully. "Imagine me thinking about all that!"

"Why shouldn't you think about it?"

Susan abruptly lifted her head. "Listen, do you have an alarm clock I could set?"

"Sure," he answered. He reluctantly stood up. "What time?"

"Six?"

The cool air in his bedroom cleared his head. Like an icy shadow crawling up his spine, he remembered why she wanted to get up early. The trade show. She wanted to investigate. She wanted to find out who kidnapped a little girl. She was going to poke around the lives of the type of people who shoot those who get in their way.

Returning to the living room, he fiddled with the knobs on the back of the old-fashioned alarm clock and asked gently, "Do you still think you have to go to the trade show? The Mounties will have it covered."

"I have to do everything I can to help Amy."

"Right. I understand that." There was no changing her mind. "Is there a back door to your building?"

"A fire door," she said, the timbre of her voice rising to a question. "But it's locked from the inside."

"Do you think you could call a neighbor to open it for us in the morning?"

"You think that's necessary?"

"No." He forced a scoff. "But it wouldn't hurt."

"You think they'll try again."

"No, I don't. But if they're watching for you, it wouldn't hurt to keep them guessing." Whoever *them* was.

Susan fingered the scrapes on the palms of her hands. "You threw a big rock at their car, didn't you? Maybe you cracked a window. We have to keep an eye open for their car. An old-model, blue Ford with paint or mud on the license plate." She shivered.

Danny regretted mentioning the back door and destroying the soft mood. "Heck, the police might have even found them by now."

"On the other hand," she said, wide awake, "someone might be camping out in front of my place right this minute, just waiting for me to come home."

Chapter Fourteen

It was very early. A hazy pink fog spread like a shroud across the road. Scrubby trees and the round tops of boulders suspended eerily above fields.

Susan's face felt stretched and dry; she missed her own bathroom with its tidy row of cleansers and moisturizers. She promised herself that the moment she got home she would put on a huge pot of coffee and have a big mug. Danny had offered to run next door to his parents' house and make her some, but she didn't want to meet someone's parents that way.

"I didn't tell you earlier—at the time I was too busy having a caffeine fit—but you look nice. Very handsome." He wore dark flannels, a white shirt, and a conservative blue tie with a thin red stripe.

"Thanks. I hated to do it, but I have to blend in with the suits."

"Hardship duty, eh?"

"The worst."

She glanced at her watch. "We're going to be just on time."

"Your friend won't forget us?"

"No, I don't think so." Susan had called Janet, a neighbor, to meet them at the fire door on the condominium complex at 7:15.

The traffic picked up and the fog thinned out as they neared the city. She tried to concentrate on practical matters: what to wear to the trade show, should she bring extra shoes in case her feet got tired on the cement floors, did she need to replenish her stock of business cards.

Danny drove onto a narrow side street. "No sense going to all the trouble of using the back door if we parade around in the open."

Susan looked up through the trees at the red stones of her building. "Park there. That alley leads to my place."

Danny pulled in, shut off the motor, and turned to Susan. "I wish you'd change your mind. I can get your stuff easily enough while you wait here."

"Thank you, Danny. But, as you said before, the chances that they're looking for me are so slim—nonexistent. Thanks, though." Besides, she thought, why should he risk his life for her? He wasn't the person who let Amy get kidnapped. She was.

"Sure." He cracked open the door.

"You can wait here, Danny."

"No way."

Taking a deep breath, Susan stepped to the exposed sidewalk, and then scurried toward the relative shelter of the alley. She stayed close to one wall. When Danny reached her, he took her hand and gave it a comforting squeeze. They hurried to the back door where her friend Janet waited.

"I've got the elevator door propped open, come on." Janet's fluffy slippers slapped over the cement floor.

"See any strangers about this morning?" Danny asked.

"No, and I kept my eyes open." She stepped into the empty elevator and stabbed a couple of buttons. She looked from Susan to Danny. "I can hardly wait to hear this story. Everybody's talking about you."

Susan said, "One day I'm a nobody, the next I'm a celebrity."

"It's not surprising people are talking about you. Did you see the lobby? Glass everywhere. Well, come up tonight and tell me all, okay? Here's my floor. See ya."

"I'll try to one day soon. 'Bye, Janet. Thanks."

Danny stared at the numbers. They slowed to a stop, the elevator shuddered, and the doors slid open. He stepped out and looked both ways. "All clear," he said, offering his hand.

"I feel like a politician with bodyguards," she answered, rummaging in her purse for keys.

The interior of her apartment looked unchanged. She reached into the fridge, pulled the coffee out, and started a pot.

"Do you have an answering machine?" Danny called from the living room.

"No, I use the phone company's service. Pick up the receiver, would you please? If it's beeping, there's a message." She heard him moving about.

"No, just the regular dial tone."

A moment later she passed a folder to Danny. "Here's the CNR annual report. You can read up while I get dressed."

"Good idea." He flipped though the glossy pages. " 'Robert Sutherland, President and Chief Executive Officer,' " he read aloud.

"That's Amy's stepfather, all right."

Her apartment looked stark, cold, and impersonal compared to Danny's warm polished wood, homemade pillows and throws, and heavy furniture. Maybe, when all this was over, she'd redecorate.

Expecting a rough day at the trade show, she selected a dark, wrinkle-proof suit and draped it over the bed. The silk blouse felt cool and airy as it fluttered down over her camisole and the lined skirt zippered snugly over her hips.

When she returned to the living room, Danny sat on the sofa with the folder on his lap. He smoothed his moustache with his index finger, his face pensive.

Susan slipped on her heels. "Did you read the CNR report?"

"Yup. I didn't realize they were into so many things. I hope we're not barking up the wrong tree."

"So do I," Susan said softly.

"Did you read the part about gold? About CNR's mineral assets?"

"Briefly."

"It's hard to believe that Cape Breton has gold—over twenty million dollars' worth in CNR holdings alone." He tapped the glossy cover. "So what's happening with this list of places? I guess they're mines?"

"The ones where gold has been discovered are being sold, same way as the offshore. Sealed bids."

"This is Crown land, eh?"

"No, some of it belongs to individuals. I tried to get Sutherland's administrative assistant, Mary MacDonald, to explain it to me, but I'm still foggy. It seems that people in Nova Scotia don't actually own the mineral on their own property."

"You mean to say, if I found gold on my land I can't sell it?"

"Apparently not. I don't know about elsewhere, but Nova Scotians own land but not the minerals in that land. The Crown reserves the right to the minerals.

You'd have to apply for exploration rights to dig in your own backyard."

"Boy, that doesn't seem right."

"Discovering gold on our own land, that's a problem I wouldn't mind having." Susan stood, ran her hands over her skirt, took a last sip of her coffee, and said, "There, I'm all ready."

The industrial end of the Halifax Waterfront held a peculiar charm for Susan. She watched it out the window as Danny's truck rolled over gravel, packed earth, and railway ties that were almost buried in the years of asphalt layers. Dingy, unadorned facades of giant buildings pushed close to the street. Between them ran narrow, paved roads that continued beside the buildings eventually to jut on hefty, oiled pylons over the harbor.

They parked with the other early birds on a sooty lot near the grain elevators and walked on foot down Water Street.

Susan read from the slip in her hand, "Building B—booth 127 to 131. That could be it. There, where those people are going inside."

"Yeah, there's a B above those doors. Not a very elaborate setup for a fancy oil exhibition."

"I haven't paid much attention, but I imagine they're also using the World Trade Center at Metro Center. That's fancy."

The air inside was cool and damp. Strips of carpet delineated the walking areas with cold, oil-stained cement between. The organizers had already set up the back and side walls of the individual displays and the exhibitors were busily filling them. A man, pushing a long, low cart, careened by.

"Sampson's booth is four rows over, about halfway down," she said.

Danny, his hands on his hips, gaped at the warehouse's towering cavern roof. "Four rows over, halfway down," he repeated. "Must be about two miles."

Susan smiled in agreement. "Big." She realized she was excited, or perhaps it was nerves. Either way, her heart raced.

"When do the public get there?"

"Another hour, I guess." She set off with Danny close behind.

"How will we ever find the CNR booth?"

Susan pointed at a giant sign being fastened to the top of one display. "We might luck out and see it, but if not, there'll be guides floating around. At these kind of things they usually set up information tables near the entrances and exits."

Two Sampson technicians worked amid a jumble of boxes, wires, cords, and tools. "Hi guys, meet my friend, Danny Shipley. Danny, this is Bob and Sandy."

Although the two did not hesitate to give Danny a friendly smile, they immediately resumed work.

Danny stepped over an open case of tools, got in the way of a trolley of boxes, and almost tipped over the not-yet-secured display sign. Finally he looked at Susan helplessly. "Anything I can do?"

"You can take the other end of this table skirt."

She handed him a corner of the pre-gathered, royal-blue material and shook it open, then they wrapped it around the long tables and tacked it in place. A half-hour later two different photocopiers hummed, the screen of a computer blinked the Sampson logo, the table was arranged with brochures, and bright posters decorated the walls of the booth.

Two other sales representatives arrived, gave the display a final once-over, and openly stared at Danny even after Susan introduced them.

"Let's go find the food concession," Susan said to

Danny who, once again, looked disconcerted with his sleeves rolled to his elbows and his hair in disarray.

She nodded to her coworkers, buttoned up her suit jacket, and led him through the crowd to the rear of the warehouse. At the end of their crammed isle was an open area of floor. Ahead was the concession. Immediately at its left the neon lights of an elaborate display spelled: *Canadian Natural Resources.*

"Wow! Will you look at that!" Danny blurted. "What a waste of taxpayers' money."

A mute group of people watched a movie on a large, flickering screen about a massive offshore oil well. On the right side of the exhibit an arch invited guests with a brilliant ENTER sign. The same-shaped arch, on the left, said EXIT ONLY.

"It looks open. Let's go in," Susan said.

Inside the twisting hall an elaborate presentation of lights and sounds instructed viewers about the history of CNR, its discoveries of oil, gas and mineral deposits, and the wealth of reserves available to Nova Scotians. Susan paused at a lit window behind which were different grades of gold-rich ore.

"I can't believe the provincial government okayed this display. It's like a sales pitch for Canadian Natural Resources," she whispered. Which seemed silly since they were about to close.

Danny grumbled, "Wish they'd put this much money into my lifeboat."

When they finally emerged from the exhibit, Susan squinted her eyes at the glare of the warehouse lights.

"Oh." She gulped, reaching her hand behind to grab Danny's wrist. "There's Sutherland. Oh! And there's Mary." She raised her hand in a tentative wave toward Mary.

A few feet away, Robert Sutherland stared at her

coldly for a beat, and then he turned to talk to a group of businessmen.

Mary MacDonald, dressed in a severe gray suit, with her hair tightly curled, wrung her hands together at her waist.

"Hi, Mary," Susan said in a light tone. "I bet you had something to do with that display we just experienced!"

A slight smile softened Mary's tired face. "Well, the ad people did most of the work, I just helped design it."

"This is my friend, Danny Shipley."

Mary shook his hand in a friendly, if distracted, greeting.

Watching Mary carefully, Susan added, "He works on the Coast Guard cutter *Seal Harbor.*"

Mary's smile hardened into a grimace. She extracted her hand from Danny's, mumbled, "Excuse me, Mr. Sutherland needs me," and walked stiffly off.

Susan looked at Robert Sutherland's back. "The poor man," she whispered to Danny. "It must be so hard for him to pretend that nothing's wrong."

"He doesn't look like he's pretending to me."

Chapter Fifteen

Susan sat on a gray metal chair and hiked it up to a
table in the concession center. After slipping off her
shoe, she massaged the ball of her foot. The shrill echo
of hundreds of voices bounced around the high ceiling
as if they were gathering speed to shoot straight through
the bones of her skull.

"What a day," she complained.

Danny, who sat opposite, prodded at the cellophane-
wrapped sandwich on her plate. "I hope you don't expect
that nutrition-free food to help. You should be eating
protein at a time like this."

"There wasn't much to choose from."

"You got that right." He carefully peeled off the plastic on a half-dozen squares of cheese. "You know, I've
been thinking. I might have been more effective sneak-
ing around the CNR booth this morning if Mary hadn't
known I was a friend of yours."

"I know," Susan said with a sigh. "I wasn't thinking

115

when I introduced you. On the other hand, it was interesting to see her reaction. Wouldn't you say she looked
guarded somehow?"

"She was uptight. But any mention of that business
you had with her boss would do that."

"Did you see anyone who looked suspicious this
morning? Anyone who made Sutherland look frightened?" She unwrapped the cellophane.

"No, not really." He chuckled. "Other than you."

Lifting the sandwich to her mouth, Susan froze.

"What? What is it?" Danny twisted his body to see
where she stared.

Susan faltered. "Those men . . . the men there . . . See
that man in the red plaid jacket? He and that other guy
were the ones in the coffee shop! They're the ones who
gave me the creeps after the first time I saw Sutherland."
She reached across and squeezed Danny's wrist. "Don't
let them see your face."

Danny jumped to his feet and wrapped his cheese in
a paper napkin. "I'll watch them, see who they talk to."

He walked with his face turned away from the ruffians
who leaned against the wall near a number of garbage
cans.

Susan did not think they had seen her so she shifted
into the seat Danny had vacated and dug into her purse.
By tilting the mirror on her compact she was able to
watch them unobserved. They looked like a couple of
laborers waiting to dismantle the show, but CORE was
a long way from over. One took a deep drag on his
cigarette and glanced to his right toward the CNR display area. After a minute Susan tired of watching them.

Her sandwich was inedible, the bread dry, the ham
curled at the edges, so she dropped it into a trash can on
her way to the nearest aisle of the long rows of displays.
She briefly considered returning to the Sampson booth,
but decided to play truant. A number of other reps had

arrived during the day, so the show would go on without her.

By the time she walked to the far end her legs and feet ached from the impact of high heels jarring on the hard cement.

The temporary guides hired by CORE's organizers sat primly behind their table. Adjusting her own nametag, she approached a pretty brunette.

"Do you happen to have a list of the companies here?"

The young woman responded to Susan's query with a toothy smile.

"Yes we do," she said, reaching for a booklet. "This has the names of the displaying companies in alphabet-ical order in the front, and at the back you'll find the booths sequentially numbered with the companies listed along side."

Susan raised her eyebrows in appreciation of the girl's spiel. "This is exactly what I needed. Thank you"—she glanced at the nametag—"Donna."

"My pleasure," Donna chirped. "Please ask if there's anything else I can do."

After taking a moment to orient herself, Susan headed toward the nearest booth. For the next couple of hours she glanced at displays, checked faces, and made small talk about CNR. But she learned nothing new. She didn't know what she was looking for and there were too many people to question. Disheartened, she returned to the Sampson booth. Her boss was there.

"Where have you been?" Gordon Moore hissed.

"Visiting potential customers," Susan said as she straightened the table.

"You have no business leaving the booth for that length of time. We need a break too."

A half-dozen Sampson employees were squeezed into the display and only one looked occupied. Nevertheless, Susan realized that her boss's anger was justified; she wasn't giving Sampson her best. But how could she? How could she sell office equipment when she knew that Amy Sutherland had been kidnapped? How could she relax until the child was safe?

"You're right, Gordon," she conceded. "I've been distracted. But I have made a lot of contacts—sales should be good this month."

A mop of blond hair caught her eye. Danny balanced on the corner of a rough bench across and down from the Sampson booth. He leaned forward, his elbows on his knees, hands hanging limply. Grateful that he had not run to her the moment she appeared—Moore would have had a heyday with that—Susan smiled at him. He shrugged, bored.

Her spirits dropped another notch. Obviously he hadn't found anything out about the men who scared her in the coffee shop the previous Monday. There had to be something she could do.

As soon as Moore was occupied elsewhere, she flitted across the corridor and plunked down beside Danny. "No luck, eh?"

"Nope." He patted Susan's hand. "They hung around there for maybe an hour, then left. I followed them outside. They got in a beat-up black car, and drove off."

"I hope they didn't see you," she said. It would be terrible if they targeted Danny.

"I also checked in with the RCMP to see if they'd learned anything new about last night's shooting."

"Nothing?" she asked.

"Nothing." He tilted her chin up and smiled. "Hey, don't look so downcast. We've still got that reception to go to."

She couldn't think of anything to say that wouldn't sound pessimistic or sarcastic so she went back to the Sampson booth and tried to work. At 5:00 she and Danny walked over to the CNR reception. In sharp contrast to the echoing activity of the trade show, quiet elegance hummed inside the Halifax Hilton. Susan gazed about the tall pillars, handsome woodwork, and potted plants until her eyes rested on the sign indicating the direction to CNR's room.

"Hope they're serving food," Danny mumbled.

"Probably. If not, there's a nice chowder restaurant down the end of this corridor."

"Well, here we are. Keep your eyes and ears open."

Susan nodded. "I just wish I knew what we were looking for."

The reception was well attended with mostly men in dark suits, but here and there women took part in the clusters of quiet conversation. The array of platters spread over a white linen tablecloth held cheese balls, cold cuts, and hors d'oeuvres.

Standing off to one side, Susan with her soda water and Danny with his juice, they surveyed the crowd. When a number of Susan's customers acknowledged her presence with a smile, she sidled over to them and introduced Danny.

"The show's doing well, isn't it?" She spoke to a forty-five-year-old balding man who was office manager of one of the largest offshore supply boat companies.

"We're busy," he said. "Halfway through the afternoon I had to send someone back for more promo material."

"Have you been through the CNR display?"

He nodded slowly, one eyebrow raised. "Pretty elaborate. They must have had money left in the coffers that they wanted to use up. You know they're dissolved as of day after tomorrow?"

She nodded. "Wonder who'll get the offshore holdings?"

"That's the question of the day, isn't it?"

Susan sipped her drink. "Will it make any difference to your company?"

"Not much, we'll get business no matter who wins the bid."

"Care to venture a guess as to who'll win?"

He rattled the ice in his empty glass a moment and looked around. "See that man?" He pointed to a tall, dignified man with steel-gray hair, coffee-colored skin, and a severely hooked nose. "I put my money on Harry Clayton there. Excuse me, will you? I want to freshen this drink. Take advantage of the free booze before I head home to the little lady."

"Sure," Susan said without taking her eyes off Harry Clayton. "See you around the show."

She decided to introduce herself to the person most likely to win the CNR tender, but when she looked around for Danny he had moved away and was deep in a conversation with a man in a tweed jacket.

Harry Clayton straightened and smiled expectantly at Susan as she approached him. Taken aback, she looked behind her thinking that perhaps he was looking at someone else.

"Susan Stead, isn't it?" Clayton said in a deep Texas drawl as he extended a hand. His smile didn't reach his eyes.

Still in a daze, she shook his hand. "Have we met?"

"No, but I've heard about you."

"How so?"

Ignoring her question, Clayton introduced himself. "I'm Harry Clayton."

"Are you in town for CORE?" she asked.

"We've been in Halifax for a number of weeks. My company has invested a great deal on the outcome of the tender on the Canadian Natural Resources' offshore holdings."

She read the tag on his jacket. "I recognize your company's name. I believe I dropped in there a couple of days ago."

He nodded. "Sampson. I have your card and folder sitting on my desk."

Susan relaxed. That would account for the fact he knew her name. Or would it? The day she called on his company, had he been watching her from some inner office without her knowledge? Did he listen to her asking questions about CNR?

She asked recklessly, "Why should you remember the name of a single sales representative when you must have dozens a week?" But before he could answer she felt a hand on her arm.

"Hello, are you enjoying the reception?" Mary Mac-Donald asked breathlessly.

"Yes, thank you," Susan stammered.

"The waiters have just brought in some hot shrimp balls that you must try," Mary said, the pressure of her hand increasing on Susan's elbow.

Clayton looked as if his attention had drifted elsewhere so Susan allowed herself to be led away from the Texan. Halfway across the room she craned her neck in time to see Robert Sutherland, his eyes ablaze, face off in front of Harry Clayton. Susan could feel the tension emanating from the circle of businessmen. Clayton and Sutherland broke from the group and stomped out of the reception room.

"Did you see that?" Susan muttered to Mary. "They looked like they hated each other."

"I expect they do," Mary answered. "His company wants to take control of the CNR projects."

"But who are they really? What background do they have?"

"Background? Gulf of Mexico, North Sea . . ." Her voice trailed off.

"Why didn't you want me to talk to him?"

"It's not that . . . I just needed a friendly face."

Susan crinkled her eyebrows when she realized Mary's hand trembled and she was unnaturally pale. "Are you all right?"

Mary heaved a shuddering sigh and whispered, as though to herself, "I don't know how much more of this I can take."

"Come on over here and sit down."

Mary shook her head and raised her chin. "I shouldn't be bothering you." Her voice turned efficient once again. "Oh look, the shrimp balls are going quickly. Here's a plate. Help yourself."

As Susan had her glass in one hand, a china plate between a thumb and forefinger, and linen napkin hooked over her baby finger, there was little she could do when Mary turned and wandered off. Finally Susan abandoned it all and went in search of Danny.

She found him before a heaped vegetable tray talking to a dark-haired man in a tweed jacket and desert boots. "Susan," he said, "meet an old school mate of mine, Rod."

"Dan said he was here with a friend," Rod said, shaking her hand, "but he didn't say it was the most beautiful woman in the room." He was handsome in a slicked-back-hair sort of way.

Danny, who had popped a broccoli flower into his mouth, made a slight choking noise. When he'd recovered, he said, "Rod's a CBC reporter."

"You're covering CORE?" she asked.

"CORE and the CNR dissolution."

"Any guesses about who'll win the tender?"

"Odds are in favor of the guy you were just talking to."

"Harry Clayton?"

Rod sneered. "Nepotism is alive and well in Nova Scotia."

Susan gave Rod her full attention. "What do you mean?"

"Harry Clayton is Robert Sutherland's father-in-law."

"But I got the impression they didn't like each other."

He shrugged. "So what?"

Susan worried her lower lip with her front teeth. Amy would be his grandchild, or would she? "Sutherland has been married twice. Is this guy his present father-in-law?"

"Yup. Deidra Sutherland, the southern belle who sold herself into the cold north."

So Clayton was Amy's grandfather. Susan thought back to the expressions on his face, the tone behind his words. He did seem anxious. In retrospect, she could see that Amy inherited her coloring from him. Itching to get away to discuss everything in private, she tried to catch Danny's eye. He was still intent on Rod.

"Why do you think the government is dissolving CNR?" he asked. "What's the real reason?"

The reporter leaned against the table and put his hands in his pockets. "They think it's a losing proposition. And it is for the short term. You've got to spend money to make money. And the provincial debt is high and they promised the voters they'd lower it. What better way to do that than to dump a company that's been carrying a twenty-six million dollar a year loss."

Susan frowned. "I have a friend who says that the fields are about to go into production, that the offshore is about to reap untold profits."

"Hey, don't we wish. The offshore is a risk. Even when they start pumping gas it'll be years before the investment is paid off."

Danny interjected, "But the mines are another kettle of fish. They've been showing a profit. No risk there."

"You been watching my show?" Rod jabbed him playfully. "I've been saying that all along. Natural resources are more than offshore oil and gas." He held up a finger at a time. "Forest, mines, fishing . . ."

Danny asked, "Are they going to announce the winners of the tenders for all the CNR holding?"

Rod shook his head. "Not on Sunday. Only offshore exploration. That's where the news is. That's where the politicians will speechify."

"When will they have a press conference to announce the other winners? Like the gold mines?"

"I doubt if they'll bother announcing them."

"But that's not right. The gold holdings alone are valued at twenty million dollars. That's taxpayers' money."

Rod jerked his head around. "Twenty million. Where'd you hear that?"

Danny shrugged. "I read it in the annual report."

"Darn, I knew I should have read that file." He shook his head. "Aw, what the heck. The public's only interested in the offshore."

Susan smiled sweetly. "Rod, do you think that if you find out anything interesting or unusual about this CNR business that you'd let us know?" She dug a business card out of her breast pocket and scribbled her home number on the back.

Rod took the card, looked at the back, and leered at Susan. She felt her face color. Danny snatched it and scribbled. "You should have my number too. We might be there. Also, give me your card so, if we hear anything, we can call you."

"What do you mean? You know something I don't?" Rod eyed Susan.

She glanced at Danny for guidance and saw an infinitesimal shake of his head.

Susan spied Robert Sutherland reentering the reception without Harry Clayton. He headed to the bar, said something, took a glass of amber-colored fluid, and drained it in one gulp.

"What's going on here?"

Susan had been staring at Sutherland but Rod's voice brought her out of her stupor.

"Hmm? Nothing," she lied.

The reporter looked ready to pounce. "Come on, 'fess up. I saw the way you were looking at him."

Danny stepped between them. "Listen, Rod, if we learn anything, we'll call you. We've got to go now. Take it easy, eh?"

As soon as they were out of earshot, Susan moaned. "I hope he doesn't pester Sutherland. The man looks like he's on the brink of a nervous breakdown."

"Funny hearing that from you, after the way he treated you."

"Well, if he's rude, at least he's got an excuse. His daughter is . . . heaven knows where."

As they left the buzzing of the reception, Danny asked, "What do you want to do now?"

"I think I want to go home. What do you say we order a pizza and eat it there?"

"Sounds good. Real good. Just give me a minute, I want to use this pay phone again and call my answering machine."

Susan leaned on the wall beside him and rubbed her fingertips in little circles over the bridge of her nose trying to dislodge the tension there. It took a moment for Danny to activate his machine. She watched the expressions flicker over his handsome face as he listened. The first message made him smile; a dimple formed on his cheek. Suddenly his eyebrows lowered, shadowing his now-wary eyes. She tensed, waiting.

Finally, he slammed the phone. "That was Rummy. Sam Spinney is drinking at the Seal Harbor Social Club. Spinney—the father-and-son fishermen. He's the guy that Rummy suspects might be the kidnapper!"

Chapter Sixteen

Danny backed the truck between two cars at the front of the Seal Harbor Social Club. It was lucky to get a spot so close; there were dozens of cars jammed in the large lot at the side and overflowing to line the road.

He switched off the key and turned to Susan. "You ready for this?"

Susan groaned. "Oh, I hope it's him."

They climbed out of the truck and walked hand in hand to the entrance. Each time the door opened, the dull throb of the sound system's bass beat seemed to puff out a swill of cigarette smoke accompanied by the twang of guitars and buzz of voices.

Inside, Danny led her across the crowded floor. He knew most of the club's patrons, the locals, so he nodded a brisk hello with every step. Susan smiled wanly whenever he introduced her. Otherwise she nervously scanned the smoky interior.

"There's Rummy," she hissed, nodding to where he

sat leaning his chair against the wall at the far end of a shuffleboard game. The two men who had shared the small round table with him listened to something Rummy said, stood, and left.

Danny, watching the retreating backs, asked Rummy, "Where'd your friends go?"

Rummy's chair was still rocked back to prop against the wall when he answered tensely, "What do ya think? I told them these seats were taken. What took you so long anyway?"

"We just got your message."

"First time I ever used one of them infernal gadgets, surprised it worked." He scowled.

Susan slid into the seat at Rummy's left. "Where is he? Where's Sam Spinney?" she asked in a hoarse whisper.

"You tell me." With his eyes fixed on hers, he repeated slowly, "You tell me if your kidnapper is in this room."

Susan flinched at his threatening tone and glanced at Danny. He found he could not look her in the eye so he stared fixedly at his hands spread on the table. If Sam Spinney was mixed up in something shady, Danny thought, he would see that justice was done. But first he needed to be convinced.

Susan straightened and scanned the packed room. She leaned to one side, to peer anxiously around a crowded table. She frowned. Danny could feel, as well as see, her collecting her courage.

With the palm of her hands flat on the table, she pushed herself into a stand then weaved her way across the floor of the bustling club. Her eyes flickered across the profile of a man who slumped facing the corner. She swung abruptly, stared across the room into Danny's eyes, and tilted her head toward the dejected-looking figure. The color had drained from her face.

"Well, that's that," Rummy said in a resigned voice. "She recognized him."

By the time Susan returned to the table, Danny was on his feet. "I'm going up to the bar. What do you want?"

"I think that's the guy. Shouldn't we call the police right away?"

"He's not going anywhere."

"But Danny, that's Sam Spinney. If he's the man I saw on the boat that night, we have to do something."

"Just let me think, would you?" Danny snapped. He immediately regretted his tone. "I'll get you a white wine."

As he fetched the drinks, he analyzed his own contradicting reaction to Susan's recognition of Sam Spinney. He should feel relief. After all, Sam might be able to lead them to the other kidnappers and, God willing, to Amy. But Danny would hate having to turn a local over to the Mounties, turning in someone who he had known, albeit not well, all his life.

He returned in time to hear Susan say, "He looks so, I don't know, morose. I feel sorry for him."

Rummy had both hands wrapped tightly about his glass. "Yup. Drowning his sorrows, all right. Wouldn't you be if you were losing everything?"

Oblivious to the humming party atmosphere surrounding them, the three put their heads close together.

"How should we go about this?" Susan asked.

He glanced at Spinney's back. "The way I see it, we've got three options. We can call the cops right now, we can talk to Sam ourselves, or we can wait and see what happens."

"There's no question about calling the Mounties," Susan said adamantly. "We *have* to do that. They'll take him in and question him."

"And if he's not the one you saw that night?" Danny snapped.

"What if he is?"

"All right. Say that he is. Say he's involved in the kidnapping. What if he's just slipped away from the others for the evening? What if he's going back to them tonight?"

"So we call the Mounties and warn them. They follow him."

"And if he uses a boat?"

"They'll follow in the cutter."

Danny shook his head. "Take too long. They'd have to go through official channels, call the rescue center and all. They'd lose him."

"I can't believe that. You could get the cutter ready, just in case."

"I can't—"

"Why not?"

"It doesn't work that—"

With a growl, Rummy interrupted, "I'll get the *Jacques II* up to steam. You follow Sam. If he goes to his boat, high-tail it to my place. We'll trail him on the radar."

Susan said, appalled, "We can't do that! We have to call the police."

Danny clutched her wrist. "We do it ourselves. If Sam's not involved, no harm done. If he is, the police are the last people we want around him right now. They'll alert him, scare him off. Then we'll never have the chance to follow him."

Danny turned to Rummy. "Any idea where he's staying?"

"With his mother, I expect. I hear tell they're gonna lose that house too."

"Lose their house?"

"Bank called in the loan."

Susan's eyes flashed. "You two are just looking out for Sam Spinney. Admit it! Amy comes second."

"Shush! Keep your voice down." Danny clutched her hand. "You're forgetting one thing. The police don't even believe this is a kidnapping. Remember how they treated you? Remember? They don't believe you."

"But after what happened last night . . . ?"

"Susan, Susan. How long would it take to get the RCMP to mount surveillance? Hmm?"

She stared at him a moment, and then looked at Rummy. She licked her lips. Finally, she nodded. "Too long."

"I'm not forgetting that little girl. If Sam does anything that proves he's involved, we'll call in the police."

"If there's even a hint he's involved," she countered.

"Okay."

"Either way," she said, "I'm going to tell DeLong about him tomorrow."

He hated to see Sam Spinney dragged into this if he wasn't already involved, but it seemed a good enough compromise. "Fair enough."

Stiffly Rummy gained his feet. "Don't you worry none. I've got me a powerful radio on the *Jacques II.* We can call for help any ol' time."

Susan moaned. "I hope we're not making a big mistake."

Rummy left.

With one eye on Sam, Danny and Susan sipped their drinks and waited. Susan's face looked pale, almost blue, in the smoky light. Danny considered asking her to stay behind. He could call his folks and get them to come and pick her up. But he knew that if he were in Susan's shoes, he'd want to take an active part.

After ten minutes Danny said, "He's almost finished that beer. Maybe we better get out to the truck."

"What if he's walking? If he's going to a boat he'll probably be walking, won't he?"

"Then we'll walk too. We can see the door from the truck. Come on."

They hurried back out to the parking lot but before they reached the truck, a man and woman waylaid them. Danny introduced the couple to Susan and then asked, "Did you see Sam Spinney in there? He's not going to try to drive home in that shape, is he?"

"I certainly hope not. He looked pretty drunk."

Danny said, "I hear he's going through tough times. Sam's not married, is he?"

"No. I don't know what happened when he was out west, but he didn't come home with anyone." She sighed. "Poor guy, all alone and all."

"Didn't I see him here a while back with a date?" Danny hadn't, but he wanted to keep the people talking a bit.

The woman raised her eyebrows. "I guess I wasn't here that night. But I heard he met a fancy city girl over at some big businessman's party."

Danny stiffened. "You mean Sutherland? That big house above the beach?"

"Yeah, he was seeing a girl who works for the guy "

"Do you know them? The Sutherlands?"

The couple looked at each other. "No, we never met them," the husband said. "Did we, hon?"

"I saw her at the grocery a couple of times. You know, buying cigarettes. She doesn't lower herself to buy her own groceries. They've got a maid. What's her name?" She thought hard. "Annie somebody—lives over Herring Cove way."

The maid. They could call her and ask about Amy, Sutherland, and Amy's grandfather Harry Clayton. "Think hard, what's her last name?"

"Now why would you be wanting to know that?" the woman drawled.

"I can't tell you, sorry."

She made a circle with her mouth. "Ohh, this is juicy. Come on, Danny Shipley, I know your mother."

"Really, I promise I'll tell you the whole story when I can. It's Coast Guard business."

"Aw, I always said you take your job too serious."

Danny reminded, "Her name?"

"Well, I can't think of it. But it seems to me my daughter knows her daughter. I'll find out and call you."

"Thanks, guys." Danny glanced up when the club door opened, but it wasn't Sam.

Joe snickered. "Anything else you want to pump us about?"

Danny rubbed the back of his neck and looked around at Susan. She stared at the club door, all the while running her fingertips in a circle on her forehead. Apparently her headache hadn't left.

"Well, let's see. Any rumors about the Sutherlands? Any gossip?"

The woman was quick with her answer. "Well, now that you mention it, I heard that their marriage's on the rocks."

"But they just got married."

"I heard they argued a lot." She shrugged.

Susan asked, "What about their daughter, Amy?"

The couple looked blankly at each other and shook their heads.

Susan persisted, "You ever hear anything about her? The little girl? Her grandfather, Deidra Sutherland's father, is an oil man from Texas."

"Nope. Poor thing though, living way up on that hill with them snobby types."

Danny couldn't think of anything else to ask them. The four of them stood looking about for a moment, like cats on a fence top, then said goodnight. Even after Danny started the motor and turned on the heater, the atmosphere inside the cab of the truck was strained.

"Danny, I've been thinking," Susan said adamantly. "I think we should call the RCMP. These people are dangerous."

"Sam Spinney's not dangerous."

"You don't know that. You said yourself he's been away and just got back into town. Maybe he changed."

"Come on Susan, we've been over this. We already decided."

He stared hard at the club door trying to calm his anxiety, and glanced at his watch every five minutes for the next hour. Susan was angry with him. Maybe he had bulldozed her into this. His shoulders sagged. His mother was always telling him that he was too bossy. He peeked at Susan. Her face looked pale and strained.

"Listen, Susan, maybe I was—" He stopped abruptly and followed her gaze. Sam staggered his way toward the road.

"He's walking," Susan hissed, and cracked open her door.

Danny had just turned in his seat when he heard tires screech in from the road. He instinctively lunged to protect Susan, but the car careened by, still gaining speed. Danny jerked in time to see it bearing down! Caught in the looming headlights, Sam hung like an animated rag doll.

Danny bellowed, "Sam! Get down!"

Two shots cracked the air! With revving engines and flying gravel, the car fishtailed out of the parking lot, straightened on the paved road, and roared off, taillights narrowing as it rocketed away.

Sam sprawled facedown on the gravel.

In an instant Danny was on his knees beside him. His face crumpled.

Sam's opened eyes looked peaceful as his lifeblood drained down his chin and into the ground. Danny put his fingers on the pulse point, the soft, lifeless pulse point. Dead.

Chapter Seventeen

Susan tried to look past her own reflection on the restaurant window to the jumble of police cars with their dome lights flashing a cold blue then blood-colored red. Though her migraine blurred her vision, she could make out uniformed and plain clothed men crouching beside, and walking about the body. Sam Spinney was reduced to a body, a victim.

Lights glared and coffee perked because the Seal Harbor Restaurant, at the front of the social club, had been taken over for the investigation center. Susan and the other witnesses had been herded inside and told to wait. No phone calls. No talking to one another. Just wait. Danny sat a few yards away with his hands dangling between his knees, his head bent. He looked sad, but too distant for her to reach even if she was permitted to talk to him.

The shooting had happened only a scant hour before, yet it seemed like more time than that had passed before the Mounties responded to the telephone call. She looked up at the sound of Staff Sergeant Mark DeLong's monotone voice. He made a moué with his lips as though he smelled something foul.

"Ms. Stead."

"Yes," she whispered, then cleared her throat.

"Take a seat through there in the kitchen. I'll be with you in a moment." He turned to confer with his associate.

Danny lifted his head and looked at her. She gave him a sad smile and threaded her way behind the counter and through a swinging door to sit alone, like an outcast in the bright tiled and stainless steel kitchen. She was dimly surprised that her hands were trembling.

The door swung open again and DeLong entered. He yanked the facing chair back roughly. "Let's get this show on the road. You're not being charged with anything, yet. But I need some answers."

"Charged? Me?"

"Okay," he started, as if on automatic pilot. "I want the whole story. Why were you here? Who was that man outside? What did you see when the shooting took place? Start from the beginning and speak slowly and clearly." He nodded toward the woman taking notes but did not introduce her.

"You know that his name is . . . was Sam Spinney?"

"I'll ask the questions. You tell your story from the beginning."

"I was on duty at CORE, the trade show, today. The company I work for has a booth." She paused. How much should she admit to? Should she tell him that she signed on at CORE only to check up on CNR? Would that make him angry? She resolved to be completely honest. "We spent the day."

"We?"

"Danny Shipley and I," she admitted. "Well, I mean,

I worked too. Demonstrated machines, made contacts. But Danny and I wanted to find out about Robert Sutherland and the CNR tender."

When Susan began to tell DeLong about the companies bidding for the offshore assets, he held up his hand. "I know all about that. Tell us about your own actions."

"We went to the CNR reception and met a number of people." She waited a beat, but he did not seem to want to know whom she met. "Then, when we were leaving Danny called his answering machine. Rummy had left—"

DeLong's eyebrows were lowered so that his eyes were deeply hooded. "Rummy?"

"Rummy . . . umm, I don't remember . . . Smith! Rummy Smith. He's a friend of Danny's. Anyway, he left a message saying that Sam Spinney was here at the bar out back." It occurred to her that Rummy was likely sitting in his boat waiting for them.

"What time was that?"

"About seven. We drove straight here."

"Why did he do that? What's Spinney to Smith?"

"Because I went to see him and, when I described the boat that abducted us, he suspected Spinney. You see, I knew that one of the older men was the father of the skipper." But DeLong knew all that. Why should she go into all that again when he and the other cops wouldn't listen to her the first time?

DeLong pursed his lips, one eyebrow raised. "Go on," he demanded.

"We drove here. I thought Sam looked somewhat like the skipper on the boat. But we didn't say anything or let him see me. We waited in the parking lot for him. He came out the door and started toward the road." She gulped and gripped the arms of the chair. "This big car kind of rushed into the parking lot—I could hear it was going fast. There were two loud cracks and everything was jumbled. I heard the car take off down the road and saw Sam on the ground."

Dropping her chin to her chest she bit on her lower lip. She did not want to cry—would not cry.

"Think hard, Ms. Stead. What did the car look like?"

She closed her eyes, trying to ignore how her heart raced, and pictured the scene. "It was big, not really new. I think you'd say a big American car; I don't know makes. But it was green or blue, dark."

Staff Sergeant DeLong asked her questions for another few minutes than said with icy calmness, "Let me get this straight. You thought that the man you saw in the club was the same one on the boat. That the victim had committed a crime. You decided to follow him and rescue this Amy Sutherland all by yourselves. Does that about sum it up?"

"Well, it wasn't like that—"

"You fools!" he barked. "You must have been out of your minds! Didn't that little episode outside your apartment teach you anything?"

"But . . . I," she stammered, finally giving up under his suspicious scrutiny.

He lowered his voice menacingly. "Or did you set the whole thing up? Huh? Perhaps that shooting, that attempted murder, was a big ruse to bring Sam Spinney out in the open? Even if you are as innocent as you claim, you're as responsible for Spinney's death as the guy who held the gun. If you had called us—as anybody with half a brain would have—he'd still be alive! So you'd better come clean. Are you in on this kidnapping scheme?"

Susan's eyes widened and her mouth hung open. She finally managed a weak, "No!" Her bottom lip began to quiver.

Still above her, DeLong placed the palms of his hands on the table and leaned his face close to hers. "Are you keeping anything else from me? Because if you are, you are in serious—and I mean accessory-to-murder serious—trouble."

There was a thump as the kitchen door was shoved back and suddenly Danny was at her side. He must have been spying through the door's gap. "Leave her alone. Can't you see she's had enough?"

"Get back with the others, Danny."

Susan clasped Danny's wrist and said, "I'm okay."

"You sure?"

She forced a smile. Danny looked from the police officer and back to Susan, and then he turned and walked back out to the dinning room. Susan grabbed a handful of paper napkins from a chrome holder and blew her nose. After a couple of deep breaths she calmed and looked DeLong directly in the eye. "I am not keeping anything from you. If you'd listened to me in the first place this wouldn't have happened."

He straightened and put his hands on his hips.

As Susan's confidence increased, a righteous anger surfaced. "I am not the criminal here! Every time you talk to me you treat me like I'm either stupid or guilty. Yes! Yes! We should have called you when we saw Sam. Yes. I admit that. But you have never given me reason to trust you—to think I could depend on you! You've treated me like I punched myself around, jumped in the ocean, and lied about ever meeting Amy."

She modulated her voice. "I'm sorry about Sam, but you should be chasing the bad guys, not yelling at me."

DeLong, ignoring her outburst, said, "You can go now but stay available at all times. I may have more questions later." With military precision, he turned on his heel and strode off. Still struggling to close her pad, his dictation officer followed.

Susan felt very weary and sad. Her shoulders sagged and she slumped in the wooden chair. Home. That's what she wanted, to go home. But Danny had driven her to Seal Harbor. She didn't have any way home unless he drove her and she couldn't ask him to do that. He'd been through enough.

"Wait!" she hollered to DeLong's back. She caught up to him. "I need a lift home, back to Halifax."

He sighed heavily and glanced at a nearby officer. The man, taking the hint, said, "I'm on my way back to headquarters. If you'd follow me." Like his colleagues, the uniformed officer was over six feet. He was young and eager to please.

"I'll be right with you."

Susan went to Danny. "That policeman is going to give me a lift home."

"Are you sure? Wouldn't you like to stay at my place again?"

"Thank you, but no." She needed time to think.

"We should talk about this, Susan."

"And we will, but I can't think straight right now. My head is splitting. I have some migraine pills and I'm going to take one and go straight to bed."

"But your apartment might not be safe."

"I'll get this policeman to check it out." He looked so distraught she kissed his cheek. "See you at the trade show."

He frowned. "You're not going back there? Not after this?"

Could she live with herself if she stopped taking part in the investigation? Abandoned Amy? It would certainly be a relief to forget the whole terrible week. But not possible. "Amy is still missing."

Chapter Eighteen

The next morning, Susan awoke and stared at her ceiling. Little Amy Sutherland . . . Time was running out. CNR's tender announcements were slated for 5:00 P.M. less than ten hours away. She worried her lower lip. The kidnappers were murderers; there was no question of that now.

She sat up straight. Sutherland wouldn't agree to do what the kidnappers demanded without some proof that his daughter Amy was alive. Why, that would mean that before 5:00 P.M. he would have to either see his daughter, or hear her voice. The murderers who shot Sam Spinney would be exposed then!

How would they arrange it? Phone probably. Could the call be traced? The Mounties probably had that angle covered. There had to be something she could do.

Dressed in a pantsuit of navy blue silk with a blouse which matched its lining, she rummaged around for a purse. When she found it she tossed in the spare set of keys from her gym bag and a few dollars from change bowls.

Danny had called her the night before, waking her from a drugged sleep, and offered to stop by to pick her up that morning but Susan had declined. She couldn't be sure what time she'd wake and the migraine medication tended to make her sleep deeply.

Thirty minutes later she parked her car at the edge of a decrepit wharf, cracked open the door, and breathed deeply. Even here, where the trains spewed their black smoke and ship's diesel engines sprayed an oily slick on the water, the salty ocean air had that wonderfully refreshing tang.

For a moment Susan shied away from stepping into the gloom of the trade show building. She firmly believed that today would be the day that Amy's fate would be resolved. Was it egotistical of her to think she could affect the outcome? Was it the height of vanity to even try?

When she strode into the cavernous building she noticed immediately that the atmosphere had changed; the early high excitement of the trade show was gone. The young temporary workers who had been hired as guides already sat in their long line behind the white draped table awaiting their first customers. Susan searched out Donna, the girl who had helped her on the first day of the show.

"Good morning." Susan smiled when Donna's face registered recognition. "How's things?"

"Fine thanks," she answered in a perky voice.

"They're keeping you busy?"

Donna waved a hand toward her coworkers. "The first day was definitely the busiest."

So, nothing exciting had happened at the show yet. At least nothing spectacular enough for Donna to notice. On parting Susan said, "I expect most people know their way around by now. Well, see you later."

The Sampson booth was deserted. The white dust covers were draped haphazardly over the equipment and tables, one corner dragged on the worn red mat. It took her a scant ten minutes to bring the display back into shape.

Up and down the aisle booth attendants waited, drinking from Styrofoam cups, sitting on top of the display tables, looking anything but professional. However, as the voices of the morning's first attendees started echoing down the corridors, they straightened their ties, yanked on suit jackets, and stood at attention beside their wares.

Craig, one of Susan's coworkers, hoofed down the aisle and took his place behind the table. "Good, the place is already set up."

"Good morning to you too," Susan replied.

He had the haughty aura of a young man recently graduated with a Masters in Business Administration: pin-striped suit, closely cropped hair, nervous, and always on the lookout for opportunity. Although she didn't know him well, since his sales territory was outside the city, she recognized that this morning his countenance was shakier than usual.

"Making rather merry last night, were you?" she teased.

His aloof stance collapsed. He grimaced. "My head's killing me. Mind if I grab a cup of coffee?"

"No, go ahead."

Susan watched his receding back, wondering if she would be able to do anything about finding Amy if she was stuck behind the table of brochures. It didn't look as though many sales representatives had signed on to work the booth that day. The CNR announcement was slated to take place at 5:00 P.M., but before then she wanted to nose around, ask questions and look for anyone suspicious.

After twiddling her thumbs for ten minutes, Susan saw Craig returning. He held a coffee in one hand and had his face buried in a newspaper. What would it say about the murder the night before? Susan didn't have long to wait. Craig sat his cup precariously on the edge of a photocopier and opened the paper across the display of brochures.

His head snapped up. "This is you, isn't it?" he asked breathlessly, jabbing a finger on a photograph.

Susan gaped. The picture had been taken when, walking beside the Mountie, she left the scene of the shooting. Shuddering, she remembered with painful clarity the exact moment of the flash.

Craig, his eyes wide, waited for her answer. Susan felt a deep bitterness at his ghoulish enthusiasm. "Yes," she almost growled, "that's me. I saw the shooting."

He was clearly anxious to hear more. "So? What was it like?"

"Listen, Craig, it was awful but I don't want to talk about it. Not yet, okay?" She definitely did not want to reminisce about the pool of blood around Sam's head or the vacant glaze to his eyes.

Disappointed, he mumbled, "Sure."

"I'm going to take a stroll around." She headed down the aisle toward the concession stand and Canadian Natural Resources' display.

It was then that she saw him in the distance. Danny. He stood off to the side, set apart from everyone around him. Not because of his height, but because of his stillness, his presence. Susan strolled over. When he saw her, Danny smiled sadly and didn't touch her in any way. She would have liked him to take her hand, or squeeze her shoulder. She guessed that he was probably very affected by the previous night.

"Are you okay?" she asked.

"Yeah, hard night, is all. How's your headache?"

"It's gone. I . . ." She wasn't sure where to start. "I feel awful about Sam."

"Me too."

"Did DeLong give you a hard time too?"

He smiled ruefully. "Yep."

"What's wrong? Have you seen those guys again? Has something happened?" She put her hand on his forearm but he felt hard and unyielding. His eyes were heavy with exhaustion.

"No, I . . . Susan, I'm sorry about not doing what you wanted last night. About not calling the police."

"You feel like it's your fault Sam was shot?"

"Of course it was."

"If he hadn't taken part in the kidnapping, it wouldn't have happened. It's not your fault; it's his own fault." She felt very certain about that.

"I suppose," he mumbled.

"Besides, he would have still been killed if we weren't there at all."

Danny nodded. "Sam was probably going soft on them or something. The others had to have been mad at him for letting you get away. They probably wanted to silence him before he went to the police with everything he knew."

Susan nodded. "That's what I think."

He seemed to brace himself. "Any ideas what we could do next?"

Susan felt a rush of gratitude toward him. He was out of his element here, on the cement floor of the trade show, but he was still game to do all he could.

"I've been thinking about the kidnappers' demands," she said. "If they have to do with the announcements of who won the exploration rights then surely Sutherland will want proof that Amy's safe before he does whatever it is they want. Don't you think he'll want to talk to her first?"

Danny nodded slowly. "I imagine the police have thought of that."

"How would that work? They wouldn't bring her here."

"Let's brainstorm ideas."

"I need a coffee for that."

They headed toward the concession stand where she purchased the coffee. Susan carefully tore away the little plastic so she could drink with the lid still attached.

Danny was looking toward the CNR display. "Suppose Sutherland found out himself who took Amy. Suppose he decided to take matters in his own hands and shot Sam?"

"He'd only do that if he already had Amy back safe and sound."

"Yup, I've thought of that. I've got my mom dropping in on Deidra Sutherland. She's going to beep me if Amy's in the house or if she sees anything at all different." He patted at the bulge of the beeper in the breast pocket of his denim shirt.

Susan felt a tremor of fear. Danny obviously adored his parents. "You sure she'll be safe?"

"Dad's going to be waiting in the truck. She's going to invite Deidra to join the Women's Institute. There's no reason for suspicion; Deidra doesn't know she's my mom."

"What'll we do now?"

He shrugged. "We could keep an eye out for those characters we saw the other day, you know, the ones who threatened you, and watch for them to make contact with Sutherland."

Susan nodded toward the CNR booth. "I can see Robert Sutherland over there right now."

"Any sign of his father-in-law? What's his name?"

"Harry Clayton. No, but I haven't looked around much."

Trying not to appear obvious, Susan swiveled in her chair and searched. "There's that reporter friend of yours. He doesn't look like he's about to go on television." Rod wore jeans and a pale blue T-shirt.

"He's probably going to change later. I'll go talk to him, see if he's heard anything."

"I'm going to walk around." She decided to patrol the full circle about the display aisles. It was a long stroll but she wore low pumps and her feet had healed since her ordeal on the shore. As she walked on the thin carpet over cement her legs jarred. She stopped every now and again and sipped on her bitter coffee. Dust motes swirled in the glare of the lights and the rumbling of voices and electrical equipment filled the air and echoed off the vaulted roof. For the entire length of the huge building she ambled along, alert but not looking anyone in the eye.

As she rounded the corner to head toward the main doors, Susan stopped short. The two thugs who had warned her off Sutherland were standing, shoulders sagged, hands in their pockets, on the far side of the table where the guides sat. Susan whirled away before they spotted her.

It appeared as if the men weren't interested in her. After all, they hadn't been lurking around the Sampson booth. Maybe whomever they worked for had other plans for them? Judging from their clothing, they weren't businessmen and if they were just there to dismantle the booths, there would be no need for them to hang around the exposition while it was running. Chances were, they had something to do with Amy's kidnapping and she meant to find out what that was.

Intent on getting into position to spy, she almost didn't notice Mary MacDonald. Mary must have seen her; she stopped moving forward and looked distressed. Susan glanced again in her direction, but she didn't take time to wave to the woman. In fact, she was relieved to see Mary do an about-face and walk quickly down the aisle.

Chapter Nineteen

The backdrop of tongue-and-groove pine, eight feet high and twelve feet long, was new. The sour smell of still-moist wood hovered in his nostrils as Danny wandered around to where the panel was braced with saw horses and grease-stained boards. As his foot brushed it, an empty soda can rattled across the cement, the sound barely audible over the din of the trade show.

"Yo, Danny! Sit on that stool, will ya?" Rod didn't wait for his response but continued fiddling with a light stand. His head leaned close to a technician.

Danny ambled up to the podium and tapped on the microphone. It made no sound.

"Stay where you are a second," Rod demanded.

The spotlights thumped on, momentarily blinding Danny. After a few seconds he could make out the shadowy forms of Rod and his camera crew setting up for the press conference. It occurred to him that politicians had to be adept at looking beyond the glare when answering questions from the floor. Would Robert Sutherland be able to look calm when it was his turn at the microphone?

"Who all is going to be here?" Danny asked in Rod's direction.

"Oh, the Premier, an MP or two, Sutherland. . . ." For a second his voice trailed off as he turned away. "Here's the advance copy of the news release."

Danny slid off the stool and took it. There were four pages of double-spaced typing. He started to read, punctuating each section by speaking out loud. "Welcoming guests . . . Closing show . . . Ah, here it is. The successful . . ." He held the paper into the air and looked to Rod with astonishment. "I don't get it."

"They've left a fill-in-the blanks where the names of the successful companies should be. It's a gimmick to add suspense."

Danny studied the page again. "But there are a lot of blank lines here."

"Sure, there'll be a lot of companies named."

"Not just one?"

"Something like this isn't awarded to one company. There are partnerships, associations, joint ventures."

"I had the wrong impression, I guess. I thought that this was a major announcement, that whatever was said this afternoon would make one person rich and leave everyone else out in the cold."

If this wasn't a major announcement, then what were the kidnappers waiting for? Why the deadline? Danny closed his eyes trying to fathom how all this affected Amy's kidnapping. It had to have something to do with the dissolution of CNR. The timing fit. The kidnappers said that they had to keep Amy alive until next week. As Susan had understood it, next week started tomorrow.

Rod shook his head. "It'll make a lot of people rich.

Or at least, give a lot of people the opportunity to make a pile of dough."

For a moment Danny jabbed at his moustache with the point of his finger. "But what about that guy, Clayton, Robert Sutherland's father-in-law? I thought he'd invested hundreds of thousands just setting up an office to bid on the offshore rights."

"He'll get a piece of it. The gamble is in how big a piece. You know that comment you made Friday night about the gold rights?" Rod continued, "I looked into that a bit. You were right; it's worth millions. Small fry compared to the offshore, but still huge."

Danny began flipping through the press release looking for the mineral section.

Rod interrupted, "Don't bother. It's not mentioned."

"They don't mention the gold ventures at all? What does that mean?"

"It means you may have stumbled onto something big. Once I saw how valuable the Cape Breton mines were I just assumed that they'd announce them tonight too." He paused for effect. "They're not."

"So you'll ask about it at the press conference? Get it out in the open?"

"Darn tootin'." Rod pulled Danny a few yards away from the working technicians. "Tell me the whole scoop, Dan—what's going on?"

Danny stared at the floor. He didn't want to do or say anything that could jeopardize Amy's chances. In all likelihood Robert Sutherland was doing all he could to see to the safe return of his child. Once she was out of harm's way, Danny thought, he would tell Rod everything.

On the other hand, there was no guarantee that the kidnappers would return Amy even after they received their payment. They had already killed once. Amy had seen their faces. She could possibly tell the police about where she had been held or at least what it looked like.

If they silenced the child, Sutherland would tell everyone what he had done. All deals would be off. Would they kill Sutherland before he found out that Amy wasn't coming home?

Danny knew the police were working undercover, although he didn't have any idea who, of the throngs around the trade show, were really cops. He squeezed his fists into tight balls.

"All right." Rod held his palms into the air in a hands-off motion. "I won't press you. It's obviously something serious. Just promise me you'll tell all when you can."

Danny's brain in overdrive had almost forgotten Rod's question. "Sure, I will, no problem."

Rod swung his arm in a wide arc. "As you can see, I'm kinda busy here so I can't call her myself. But I know this girl who is a secretary at the Department of Mines and Energy. It occurs to me that she might know if the names have been changed yet on the gold properties. You know they have to register the titles. Want her number? Want to call her yourself and ask?"

Danny felt a burst of adrenaline. Something positive to do finally. "It's Sunday. I'll have to call her at home. Give it to me. Thanks."

Ignoring the startled looks that followed him, Danny jogged to the pay phones at the front of the building. He had some trouble explaining to the woman on the other end of the line who he was—she didn't remember ever having met a CBC reporter named Rod—but she finally understood his question.

"Well, yes, it's already been done," she said. "I worked on it myself. You see, except for the names that were put forward for the valuable properties, the titles revert to the original landowners."

"Can you remember any of the names of the titles that changed hands?"

"No." She sounded apologetic. "Nothing seemed out of the ordinary."

Exasperated, Danny asked, "So nothing said or done in tonight's press conference could change what was done in your office on Friday?"

"Well, sure, the government—I guess in this case that would be Mr. Sutherland—he could announce another name. Say, if there was a gold mine that had some commercial viability he didn't know about before, he could register the mineral and property title for that tonight. But that's highly unlikely, I mean, he'd know if there had been a significant discovery, wouldn't he?"

"Let's just say, for the sake of argument, that this afternoon gold was discovered in one of the nonproductive mines currently under lease by CNR. Then tomorrow, after those CNR leases have expired, who would have the right to dig up the gold and sell it?"

"The original owners of the land. If the mines are thought to be unproductive, the rights will revert to the original owners tonight at midnight."

Tonight at midnight. "And the only way that could be stopped?"

"Would be for the find to be announced before midnight tonight."

"Thank you," Danny breathed the words. "Thank you very much."

He hung the receiver and leaned his back on the wall staring vacantly toward the busy trade show, his mind clicking over the implications. What if someone owned land that had gold on it, say a find worth many millions of dollars, but the discovery was kept a secret? The owners wouldn't want CNR to know about it because then they wouldn't get the rights to mine that gold. What if Robert Sutherland *did* know about the discovery? Could the owners have taken Amy to keep Sutherland from announcing the find?

Danny reached into his pocket for another quarter to phone DeLong. Once he'd told the RCMP officer about his theory he would search out Susan.

Danny didn't realize that, at that moment, Susan wasn't far off. She was still trying to avoid being seen by the two ruffians whom she suspected of being in on Amy's kidnapping. Still hiding behind three men who were walking to the main doors to the left of the pay-phones, she angled herself toward the desk of guides.

The girl she had spoken with that morning had her back to her, but Susan didn't dare move around the table because then she would be facing the ruffians.

"Donna," she whispered.

Donna turned around. The quizzical look on her face transformed into a smile. "Hello again."

"Will you please do me a favor? I need to find out about the two men behind me. See them? Over by those metal stairs? One has a red-and-black jacket on. They're both wearing jeans."

Donna peered around Susan. "Yes, I see them."

"Can you think of any excuse to talk to them? I want to know who they are without them seeing me."

Donna pursed her lips then grinned conspiratorially. "Sure. I've got a survey form here. It's for complaints but they don't need to know that."

"Oh, that's perfect!" Susan pointed. "I'll be over by that booth."

Susan hung the strap of her bag on her left shoulder so she could turn her body away from the men and pretend to dig inside. She scurried into a display that was obviously not doing much business. The only attendant looked up from his papers confused.

"Sorry." Susan waved him back to his reading. "Just ignore me."

She hid behind a painted mural of gadgets, tubes, and gears, standing too close to get a sense of its purpose. Only for an instant did she worry about how suspicious she looked, peeking around the corner.

Donna was closing in on the target. The men watched with interest as she approached; she was a pretty girl. Susan couldn't see her face but Donna's head bounced back and forth as she spoke and she occasionally scribbled on a clipboard held high to her chest. The normally somber men were smiling.

Susan, with one eye around the corner of the display, watched intently, taking short shallow breaths. Long minutes passed. It occurred to her that she should be telephoning the police. If only Danny were with her, he could be doing that while she waited.

At the light touch on her elbow Susan jerked and hit her shoulder on the mural. It wobbled.

"I'm sorry—" Mary began, but Susan interrupted.

"No, no. That's all right." She checked that the mural stood firm and peeked about the corner. Donna had finished the interview. Susan knew she looked suspicious so she confided to Mary in an excited, playful voice, "I'm spying on those two men over there."

Mary's eyes flicked behind Susan's shoulder. "Why?"

"They were rude to me in a coffee shop one day. I want to know who they are and what they've got against Sampson reps." She felt uncomfortable about talking to Mary about this, but what choice did she have? Her own reputation meant nothing in the face of the danger Amy was in.

Donna arrived, scurried out of the men's sight, and reported, "They're from Cape Breton." She glanced at the clipboard. "The one in the green vest is Mike MacLeod. He's unmarried, works in a coal mine. Looks it too; his fingernails were gross. The other one's name is Charlie Dunlop." She preened. "He opened right up to me, even showed me pictures of his wife and kids."

Mary moved abruptly and knocked against the display table. Metal parts rattled precariously on the edge. Throwing Susan an embarrassed glance, she said, "I'm such a klutz today. See you around." And she backed away.

"Mary, wait," Susan said, but Mary strode off.

"Boy, she's a nervous wreck," Donna said.

Susan mumbled, "Yes, she pretty much put this show together, must have been quite a strain." She debated about going after Mary.

As she checked to see that the two men hadn't moved, Susan caught a glimpse of Danny's straw-colored hair. The crowd about him thinned and he became more visible. Susan pointed. "See that man with the blond hair?"

"The cute one?"

"Hmmm." He *was* cute. "Would you bring him to me?"

Donna jibed, "Why should you get him? I think I'll keep him for myself."

"Very funny," Susan said. "Just go get him, please. I can't step out there, the Cape Bretoners will see me."

While she waited, Susan peered down the aisle in the other direction looking for Mary. Ever since she had first met her, she had been acting bizarrely. The effort of producing a show like CORE was no doubt horrific. Not only that, she had lost her job. And her boss, someone she may or may not have very strong feelings about, was fighting to get his child back. But Susan suspected there was even more to it than that.

Danny appeared. Susan grabbed him and hauled him behind the mural.

"I've got to get back to my table," Donna said regretfully. This was clearly more fun than touring people around CORE.

Susan said, "Yes, yes, of course you do. Thanks for all your help." Donna edged away backward, her eyes on Danny.

As soon as Donna was out of hearing range, Susan blurted, "Those guys are back—see them? The red-and-black-checked jacket?"

She thumbed in their direction without looking. They probably didn't know Danny's face so there would be no harm in his open scrutiny.

"And the other one in a vest. Yeah," he answered tensely.

"I got Donna to talk to them. They're from Cape Breton. Mary was here and she got really jumpy when Donna told me who they were. Do you think she could be involved?" She had been one of the possible suspects running through her mind, but until now it seemed so unreal, so unlikely.

Danny, who had been watching the men, yanked his head about. "That makes sense," he said fervently. "I've got a theory," and he related his telephone call with the woman from the Department of Mines and Energy.

"So you think that's the motive for the kidnapping?"

"It would mean that Sutherland knew about a gold discovery but was warned to keep his mouth shut. That the kidnappers are the original owners of those mines. If we could find out who they are we might find out where they've got Amy."

"You mean check if any boats in Seal Harbor are registered in the same name or something. But that would take too long."

"These guys aren't that stupid."

"I wonder how Mary fits in. Does she know them? If that's the case, she's in it up to her eyeballs. We've got to tell DeLong."

Danny grunted. "I just talked to him. Told him about the gold discovery theory."

Susan felt a fool. "Mary probably told those guys to follow me into the coffee shop. Hey! Why did she steer me clear of Harry Clayton at the reception on Friday?"

"He's Amy's grandfather. Maybe he doesn't even know she's missing. Or, more likely, Sutherland was worried that Clayton would do something to upset things. All along he's probably been planning to do whatever the kidnappers want—anything to get Amy back."

"I think Clayton does know everything. Otherwise he and Robert Sutherland wouldn't have been arguing." Susan stopped abruptly. "Peek behind there. Are those guys still there?"

Danny leaned slightly to look behind the mural then, with a jerk, stepped into the aisle. "I can't see them."

"What are we going to do now?"

"You call DeLong and describe them. Give him their names."

"Good idea."

"I'm going to try to find them."

"Okay," she clipped over her shoulder. "Ask Donna; she might have seen which way they went. Meet back at the Sampson booth?" Scanning openly, Susan strode onto the cement floor in front of the main doors.

"Right."

Danny determinedly strode off.

When Susan phoned her message into DeLong he listened carefully and said, "I've got two men there. I'll bring them up to date."

"Get one of them to meet me at the Sampson booth," she suggested. "I can point them out to him."

"That's not a good idea," he said patronizingly. "My men are working covertly for a good reason."

As she hurried back to the Sampson booth, Susan couldn't refrain from searching the faces of everyone she saw. Probably an undercover officer trailed her—an eerie but not unpleasant notion.

At her own booth she saw Craig deep in conversation with Gordon Moore. She sighed deeply, braced for a conflict, and said, "Things are pretty quiet, eh?"

At the sound of her voice both men jumped to attention with eyes wide and smiles forced. They'd obviously been talking about her. Moore darted a glance at the table before them and Susan, following his look, saw the newspaper story with her photograph. So Gordon also knew she'd been questioned regarding a murder.

"Well," she said sarcastically, "I'm glad to see you're not run off your feet."

"Yeah, well," Craig fumbled his words. "Ah, these shows are a waste of time." Blinking at Moore, he stammered, "Ah, that is, what I mean is . . ."

Gordon Moore, the boss who had been an exasperating thorn in her side, now refused to meet her eyes. She sidled up to him and a muscle in his cheek twitched. She reached in front of him for the paper and he took a nervous step backward.

Gordon cleared his throat. "Um, Susan, Craig and I may as well go for a lunch break."

She hesitated, afraid to be trapped there. Amy's safe return was more important than the manning of the Sampson booth.

A soft, girlish voice saved her from answering. "Excuse me, Ms.—?" Donna, the guide, grinned impishly. "That man, the one you asked me to get for you before, well, now he's asked me to get you and bring you to him."

"Oh! Oh, great!" Susan turned to her boss. "Sorry guys, this is important."

Wide-eyed, Donna nodded agreement. "He said to hurry."

They took off down the aisle, Susan with forceful long strides and Donna with a scurrying gait.

"Where is he?" Susan asked. She didn't want to plunge headlong into the two Cape Bretoners.

"Right up front. He's watching the same two men that you did and they're sitting on those metal stairs that go up to the offices." Puffing for breath, she hurried on. "What's this all about? Is it a game?"

Without losing stride Susan glanced at her. "It's like a game."

As they neared the front of the building Susan slowed her step. She glanced behind hoping to see a police officer in tow, but the only people looking her way stood at a nearby display table.

Donna had gone ahead. "They've left!" she wailed. Disappointed she hurried into the open space at the front.

Susan's shoulders sagged. "Left?"

Donna pointed toward the long tables where she and the other temporary guides had been stationed. "Yeah, he was over there and"—she swung her arm—"the men were up there."

"Which way did they go?" Susan asked. "Maybe those girls would have seen them?"

Donna scurried up to the table and said, "You guys know that cute fellow who was talking to me before? The blond one? See where he went?"

"Out," they spoke in unison. "He just left."

Susan frowned. He must have followed the Cape Bretoners outdoors. She smiled a quick thanks to the guides, waved at Donna and hurried out the main doors.

For an instant she was blinded by the sunlight. After hours spent in the cavernous warehouse everything seemed unreal. She scanned the area. Two workmen in striped railway overalls strolled down narrow Water Street. A small car slowed as it approached them, then, realizing they wouldn't make way, swung onto the opposite side of the street to pass. Then, except for the buzz of city traffic a few blocks off and the humming of the nearby container terminal, it was quiet.

The warehouse, like many more along the docks of Halifax, had been built with one end jutting over the water so that boats could unload close to the giant cargo doors. Susan walked to the north corner of the warehouse and peered down its long length to where the harbor sparkled.

A tug was tied alongside the wharf, its deck a few feet lower than the wooden platform. Such a massive building, Susan thought, and yet no sign of life except the bobbing up and down of two gray-and-white seagulls on the water.

Where could Danny be?

Susan considered walking all the way down to the far end. But what if he wasn't there? Starting to panic, she looked back toward the main doors just in time to see Mary MacDonald emerge.

The woman paused, adjusting her eyes to the bright light, giving Susan time to spin out of sight behind a stack of barrels. Then Mary turned and, her hands clutched in front of her and elbows splayed to the side, walked stiffly to the south corner. As she disappeared around it her head swiveled as though she looked for someone.

Susan immediately determined to follow her but fretted about telling Donna to let Danny know. No time. She sprang from her hiding spot and, with a stiff-legged, speed-walking gait, hurried in the direction Mary had gone.

Chapter Twenty

Along the south side of the warehouse was a stretch wide enough for a vehicle to pass carefully over wooden boards as long as its tires rolled close to the rough square timbers that formed an insignificant barrier to the murky harbor waters.

Mary, sticking to the safety of the building, moved in a jostled, awkward run with her head jammed into her shoulders and her arms straight at her side. The wind caught her hair so that it stuck out in wiry disarray.

Disregarding the fact there was no cover to hide behind, Susan followed. Halfway along Mary stopped and leaned forward from the waist, her hand clutching her side. Susan had an anxious moment but, without looking back, Mary started up again. When she reached the end of the building Mary angled away to the left and out of sight. Susan sprang into a jog, quickly covering the distance between them, then flattened against the wall and peeked around the corner.

At the very end of the wharf Charlie, the Cape Bretoner, still in his red-checked shirt, stood with his back to the harbor, his eyes on Mary.

Gusts of wind off the water picked up a length of packing twine and tumbled it across the wood and high above two seagulls argued with piercing cries. Mary didn't slow her pace. The instant she reached Charlie her knees buckled slightly and he caught her by the elbows. Their bodies touched full-length.

Charlie pushed Mary off and stepped away. She held her palms up in a pleading gesture but he seemed to bristle. Something he said shocked Mary. She half-stumbled, her hands flat against her face. He walked about her like a cocky rooster while she seemed to shrink in size.

Susan crouched in a starting position, checked that they looked away, then scurried a couple of yards to hide behind two barrels. She pulled herself into a tight ball and listened intently.

"You can't be!" Mary wailed.

"Oh shut up and come on."

"No," Mary snarled. "I'm not going anywhere with you."

"Listen, you old . . . Mary,"—his voice became lower, more threatening—"we'll talk about this later."

"There won't be a later. You killed Sam, didn't you? Didn't you!"

He swore violently. "You're coming with me."

Hearing Mary's shrill cry, Susan looked over the top of the barrel. Charlie hauled Mary by the arm. When she kicked at him he raised a hand and struck her soundly across the mouth. The smack echoed. She stumbled and landed hard on one knee.

Susan flung herself across the wharf. Charlie half-turned and grunted as she straight-armed him with her full weight. As he struggled to right himself, Charlie rammed Susan's shoulder. She spun around colliding with Mary.

Mary's face registered the shock as she tumbled back toward the water. Even before the sound of a splash, Charlie hightailed it away. From the corner of her eye Susan saw a blur go after him. It was Danny; he'd come out a small rear door.

"Mary?" She crawled on her knees to the edge and peered below where Mary sputtered and thrashed, panicked.

"Hold on." Susan yanked at her suit jacket, kicked off her shoes, and poised to dive in. *Umph!* Hands grabbed her. She turned swinging. It was Danny!

"He got away," Danny said, still panting for breath. "He had a car waiting just down there." He thumbed in the direction where Charlie had run. Then, glancing down at Mary, took a couple of side steps, leaned forward, palms flat on the wood, and deftly swung his legs over.

Susan kneeled on the rough wood and watched his head descending. Mary wasn't in any danger; she simply needed Danny's calming voice to direct her toward the ladder. A moment later he coaxed her to follow him, hand over hand up the rusty metal bars, and over onto the wharf where she collapsed in a sobbing bundle.

Susan dug into her purse, hauled out a handful of tissues, and handed them to Mary. They immediately shrank to a soggy mess in her wet hands but she applied them to her running nose anyway.

"How did you know where we were?" Susan asked Danny.

"I followed Charlie. What are you doing here?"

"I followed Mary."

He smiled and their eyes met in a fleeting but understanding gaze.

Danny hitched up the knees of his trousers and

dropped to a crouch beside Mary. She looked pathetic, her skirt hoisted halfway up her thigh, hair stuck to her face, mascara smudged in half-moons below her eyes.

Susan sat on the raised timber bordering the wharf and said gently, "It's okay now, Mary."

"Leave me alone!"

Susan tried again. "Would you like me to go get Mr. Sutherland for you?"

Mary shrank from her. "Oh no! Oh this is awful! He lied. He said he loved me. But he lied!"

Susan felt at a loss. "Who lied? Robert Sutherland?"

Mary shook her head violently and blew her nose.

Susan glanced at the open door to the trade show, praying she'd see a policeman there, but there was just an impression of people moving around inside.

Danny looked at Susan. "We're running out of time."

She nodded at him. "Mary," she said, fighting to keep the anxiety from her voice, "what's going on?"

"Leave me alone! It's your fault!" She kicked her feet toward Susan like a child throwing a tantrum.

"Mary, think about Amy for once!"

"How could this happen to me?" Mary wailed.

Susan snapped. "How dare you feel sorry for yourself! What about Amy? A little four-year-old!"

Danny placed a restraining hand on Susan's forearm and said coldly, "That's right, Mary. We want some answers and we want them now."

Mary's bottom lip quivered. "They won't hurt her," she whispered between sniffles.

Susan felt every nerve in her body grow cold. "Who won't hurt her?" More loudly, "*Who* won't hurt her?"

Danny whispered, "Let me."

Susan leaned back on her heels and gulped in quieting breaths. Danny put his hand on Mary's quivering shoulder.

"Shush. Mary, it's over now. The important thing is

to get Amy home safe and sound. You understand that now, don't you, Mary?"

"But they won't hurt her," Mary whined. "They said they wouldn't hurt her."

"Your talking about Charlie, aren't you, Mary?"

She nodded. "He's not a bad man. He wouldn't hurt a flea."

Susan cried, "Wouldn't hurt a flea! They shot Sam Spinney! He's dead. Stone-cold dead. For pity's sake, where are they holding Amy?"

Mary sobbed, "I can't tell you!"

"You have to. Where are they keeping her? Tell us!"

Mary slumped limply, and her face looked full of self-pity. Danny knew if they didn't get her to open up soon she would withdraw into silence. He fixed Susan with a meaningful stare. "Go get some help."

She licked her lips and nodded. He could hear her heave a shuddering sigh as she headed back into the building. Mary sat up straighter and rearranged her soggy skirt about her legs. Her shoulders rose and fell with each breath.

Placing the tips of his fingers under her chin, Danny tilted Mary's tear-ravaged face toward him. "You're in an awful mess, eh Mary?"

She sniffed and her face crumbled.

"Hold on. Hold on." He waited for her to calm before continuing, "The only way you can save yourself is to help the police. Hmm? You know that if they hurt Amy you'll go to prison for a very long time? Prison."

"They won't." She sounded unconvinced. "Why would they hurt her?"

"Why not?"

"Well, Robert said that he wouldn't cooperate unless they proved that they didn't hurt her."

"When are they going to let him see her?"

"He can't see her. They're going to let him talk to her on the phone."

"When?"

"Just before the press conference." She spoke very softly, her eyes slightly glazing.

"Robert Sutherland told you that?"

"No!" She jerked her head back. "He doesn't know."

Danny prompted her, "He doesn't know you're a part of it?"

She said adamantly, "I'm *not* a part of it. All I did was deliver the demand note. Honest. I hung around when they were planning it and stuff, but when they asked me to do things I usually said no even though it made Charlie mad at me."

"But you knew about them shooting Sam," he persisted.

"No I didn't! I put them on to Sam and his dad. I knew Sam was selling drugs when he was out West so he'd be interested. But I never dreamed they'd shoot him. You've got to believe me!"

"Okay, okay," he said soothingly. "But you know what's going on. You know that Amy is going to be somewhere where she can talk to her dad on the telephone. Where is she going to be when she telephones?"

Danny could hear Susan screaming inside the building. "Police! Someone, get the police! We need help here!"

Mary shook her head violently. "I'm not saying anything more. I'm leaving now." She attempted to rise, her knees trembling violently, but Danny held her still with a firm hand on her shoulder.

"They'll kill her, you know that, don't you?"

"No, no, no."

"They will. They'll kill Amy because she can identify them. They'll kill Sutherland. And," he finished menacingly, "they'll kill you."

She turned frightened eyes to him. Danny could see her struggling with her conscience. Finally she said in a rush, "No they won't. Robert doesn't know who they are. And Amy's only a little girl; she won't say anything. And I'll . . . I'll go away."

"Mary! Stop and think! Charlie doesn't need you or Sutherland after tonight. The gold mine will be in his name—his alone."

She whispered, "How did you know that?"

Danny persisted. "We know all about discovery of gold in the mine in Cape Breton. So you see, your only hope is to tell us where Amy is."

Mary dropped her head back so her mouth gaped open.

"Mary, look at me. Where is Amy right now?"

"Oh, what's the difference." Her eyes rounded when he tightly squeezed her shoulder. "They've got her in a cabin on some island in Terence Bay. They're going to put her on the boat to call ship-to-shore this afternoon."

Footsteps shook the surface of the dock. Danny glanced past Mary to the people who spilled from the warehouse and surrounded them. One young man, crew-cut hair, brown tweed jacket, pushed his way to the front and thrust a badge forward. Danny grabbed his arm and dragged him clear of the crowd.

"I'm the skipper of the Coast Guard cutter *Seal Harbor*. Did DeLong mention me?"

"Yes." The young officer nodded.

"Get on your phone and call the Rescue Center. The kidnapped girl is somewhere in Terence Bay but she'll be on a boat calling ship-to-shore sometime before five. Tell them to get the Seal Harbor cutter fired up; I'm on my way."

"Got it!" He pulled a cell phone from his pocket and, striding quickly to a quiet spot a few yards off, started speaking.

Danny knew he should be running to his truck. Even after they got to the cutter, they still had an hour to reach Terence Bay. He had to be out on the water when the kidnappers made the call to Sutherland, had to be able to close in on them fast. He bounced up and down on the balls of his feet to look over the heads of the people and spied Susan. She caught sight of him at the same moment and her face broke into a nervous smile.

"Terence Bay," he yelled.

A moment later they were running hand in hand down the side of the warehouse. Five minutes later they sped around the Armdale Rotary and headed toward Spryfield. Danny leaned forward, his face near the windshield, and stomped on the gas pedal. Out of the corner of his eye he saw Susan brace her arm on the dash.

"What did Mary say?" she asked, and then grunted as they bumped over a hole.

"They've been holding Amy on an island—apparently they have to use the ship-to-shore when they want to telephone."

"Did she say Amy's okay?" she asked anxiously.

"They're taking her out on the boat this afternoon while they contact Sutherland. Mary said they'd let Sutherland talk to her before the press conference, so they're probably leaving about now."

"Taking the boat out? Why do that? Why not just use the radio without leaving dockside?"

"Don't know. Maybe they want to be mobile. Maybe they're hiding on an island that doesn't have a clear line-of-sight for VHF and they haven't updated their communications."

The car in front of them stopped to let another turn the corner. Danny tapped an agitated finger on the steering wheel. "Should we have waited for the police. Their car'd be faster." He pressed the heel of his hand on the horn. They started up again.

"What time is it?"

"Three-ten."

Danny's worst fear was that the kidnappers would let Amy stay on the line only long enough to convince Sutherland that she was alive, and then they'd get rid of her. He shuddered at the visions that induced and hoped Susan hadn't picked up on his train of thought. Her brows were knit as she frowned out the window.

"I hear a siren!" Susan craned her neck to look out the back window.

Through his rear view mirror Danny saw an RCMP cruiser appear around a curve. He braked and shuddered to a stop on the gravel shoulder. The police car, sirens stilling momentarily, pulled along side. Staff Sergeant DeLong called out the passenger window, "Get in!"

Danny jammed the shift into park, yanked out the keys, and scrambled into the cruiser's back seat. Susan landed beside him. The vehicle started away before she slammed the door.

"The cutter's ready?" Danny yelled over the blare of the siren.

DeLong said, "As far as I know."

"Check, would you?"

"It'll be over the police band, the kidnappers might hear it."

Delong was right about the public monitoring the police band, but speed was vital. "So pretend we've got a boat needing assistance."

"Right."

At a sudden thought, Danny put his lips next to Susan's ear. "I hope Rummy heard the radio and figured out what's really happening. We could use his help."

Ahead the sky was a solid white color, fog over the Atlantic. That wasn't a bad thing. The cutter's equipment would be much superior to the old fishing boat—assuming they still used Spinney's—and they could stay hidden in the fog until they were practically on top of them. Then what? Danny didn't know.

DeLong, who had been speaking into his radio, hollered back, "We're wondering about calling in a helicopter? Lands and Forests can get one here in under an hour. Search and Rescue's tied up."

"I suppose it wouldn't hurt to have them hovering nearby," Danny said. "Tell them to stay clear until they hear from us. Best not to alert the target, best to keep them feeling safe."

"What's happening back at CORE?" Susan asked.

"They arrested the woman."

"And Amy's father?"

"He's in protective custody. They're postponing the whole announcement thing until things get sorted away."

Susan smiled grimly. No matter what happened, the kidnappers weren't going to get their gold.

Suddenly they were at the Seal Harbor Coast Guard Station. As the car squealed into the parking lot, the siren popped off but the sound echoed slowly away. Harkey waited on the cutter's deck. Danny breathed a sigh of relief. The gray-haired deckhand, as fun-loving and easygoing as he appeared, was sensible, fearless, and quick when confronted with an emergency.

He bounded from the car, sprinted across the drive and dock, and leaped on board. Taking the wheel from the other deck hand he glanced around. The engine thudded beneath his feet, the radar bleeped at his elbow. Ready. "Okay boys, cast off."

He didn't check to see if Susan was safely on board because it was now or never if they hoped to find Amy Sutherland alive.

Chapter Twenty-One

There wasn't much rocking, just a tilting sensation, but Susan held onto the sturdy pipe frame with a tenacity that could withstand a capsize. She realized this and smiled grimly. Danny had told her that the Coast Guard cutter *Seal Harbor* was self-righting, could flip completely over and would still bob up straight so, if she held on tightly enough, she would come up too. She would rather not put it to the test.

She tried to relax, breathed in deeply, and felt the cool, foggy air wash over her.

Harkey, who moved agilely despite his gray hair and lined face, squatted beside her. "How's it going, eh?"

"Hi." Susan smiled and raised her eyebrows. Her hair, buffeted by the wind, slapped her face.

"You look cold. I'll go get you a slicker."

She had thought that it was the tension making her muscles rigid and her shoulders hiked to her ears, but he was right. She consciously relaxed and released one hand from the pipe. When Harkey returned with the bright-yellow jacket, Susan hid her nervousness, stood, and slid it on.

The cutter was well out into Seal Harbor now. The mist partially obscured the view as the government wharf grew smaller in the distance. On the boat's left, densely packed softwood trees sloped gently to the gray, rock shoreline.

Susan turned her attention back to Harkey. "How long do you think it'll take to get there?"

"The skipper says we're headed to Terence Bay so, aw gee, I figure about an hour, maybe less. We're going at quite a clip."

Susan, now sitting on the raised portion of the aft deck, braced her feet. An hour seemed a long time. She just wanted to get to Amy.

"Well, I'd best get back inside and see if the skipper needs me. You can go below if you want, it's warmer down there."

"I think I'll wait here a while. Thanks for the jacket," she said as he sauntered off.

Danny had his back to her, but she could see him through the opening to the bridge. He had his hands on a large, white steering wheel, like one in a car, and faced a jumble of equipment—dials, small boxes, glass domes, levers, knobs and screens. He faced an insignificant-looking rectangular porthole.

The cutter tilted again as they pulled toward the open ocean. Because of the fog, the horizon line was only the spot where the darker gray of the fog-shrouded water changed to a lighter gray of the sky. It was damp and cold and the wind buffeting her ears made her feel like she was in a noisy tunnel.

Five minutes later Danny startled her by dropping a rough gray blanket over her shoulders. "You okay back

174 Lynn M. Turner

here?" he asked, tucking the blanket around her like a papoose.

"Oh, that's nice. Thanks. Oh! Who's driving?"

"Harkey."

"I wish it didn't take so long."

"Me too. Listen, Susan, you know you'll have to go below in a few minutes, where it's safe. I mean, you shouldn't really be on board. It's against regulations."

"Okay."

"You're not seasick, are you?"

"No, I don't think so." She did feel slightly woozy but thought it was just nerves.

"I just wondered why you were staying out here, that's all."

She waved a hand, palm up, to indicate the view. "I don't get to see this too often."

The fog blanketed the shore with shades of gray-blue. A fine white line shimmered where the surf hit the rocks and pale crescents of sandy beaches.

Danny's face lifted in pride. He nodded to the aft where the Seal Harbor Island Lighthouse swung its beam. "I've got a little sailboat. I'll take you over there sometime, over to the light."

"That'd be great."

Susan stared at him in frank admiration. He looked vibrant and manly: the salt spray in his hair, his muscles taunt yet totally attuned to the movement of the cutter, his eyes a vivid blue.

"Yo, there's a blip here on the radar!"

"Coming," Danny hollered then said, "Don't worry, it won't be them. Likely just a fishing boat."

A couple of sure leaps him brought him inside. Susan staggered after him. Inside the men watched the radar screen. The bridge was as crowded as an airplane's cockpit.

Danny was saying, "I don't like to use the radio. From

this position it'd be like announcing ourselves to the target."

DeLong asked, "You don't think this is them?"

"No. I don't think they'd come this far out of the Bay. No need."

"So we ignore them?"

"I think that'd be best."

DeLong mumbled, "I'm going below to confer with my boys," and, as he lowered his solid frame down the four-foot ladder into the cabin, added, "Inform me the instant you see something."

Danny grunted at him then said to Susan, "Come on over here." He pointed at the radar with two fingers tight together. "This is us right here in the middle. The land is red and the shore is yellow. That red dot, that's the boat we're talking about."

Susan adjusted her thinking to the two-dimensional screen. A line, radiating from the center, swung around— beep, beep, beep. It looked like they moved slowly off shore, an island directly ahead. To confirm, she peered out the porthole and saw its hazy gray-green outline like an overturned bowl.

"That red dot seems to be going in the same direction as us," she said anxiously. "Do you suppose it's them? They could have already made the call and be going back to their hide-out."

Danny licked his lips, glanced toward the cabin, and said very slowly, "I don't think it's them. Nope, I don't think it's the kidnappers." He turned his attention to the instrument panel with a curious expression on his face, eyebrows frowning, lips smiling.

"But there's no other boats in the area," Susan persisted. When he threw her a meaningful look and tapped a vertical finger to his lips she mouthed the name, Rummy? He raised his eyebrows and shrugged.

Susan studied the radar. "So we're not near to the kidnapper's boat yet?"

Danny flicked another look from the front portholes to the radar. "It's hard to tell around all these rocks and islands. You see, if they're close to shore, it's hard to tell the difference between a boat and a shoal."

A while later, DeLong spoke from the opening into the hull. "Anything?"

Danny nodded. "Better get your boys deployed out on the deck now."

Two huge officers, jackets removed and holsters unobstructed, climbed up the stairs. Susan stepped outside to make way. Once they were free of the bridge she jumped inside and clambered down the ladder-like steps into the small cabin where Harkey leaned over a table studying a chart. Danny had told her that she should go below, that according to regulations she shouldn't be on board at all, but the restriction chafed. It was like being in the furnace room of her apartment building—dark, cramped, loud, and throbbing. And there were no portholes so she wouldn't be able to see what was going on. She sat stiffly on a bench, her hands clutching the chilly plastic and her feet braced against the boat's movement.

Harkey pointed to a section of the chart. "I'm trying to imagine just where in heaven they could have been hiding around all this mess."

Susan darted an anxious glance at the chart. "When we find them, will we be able to catch them?"

"If they don't get themselves lost around those islands first."

"Can the helicopter follow them and tell us where they've gone?"

"Too foggy."

"The radar?"

"Up to six or seven miles and only if they haven't taken too close to the shore and—"

Suddenly Danny hollered from above, "Harkey!"

Harkey sprung away, reached up to the ceiling, clutched a bar, and pulled himself into the bridge. Immediately the drone of the engines changed pitch, slowing. She stood at the foot of the steps peering up at the three pair of legs shuffling by.

Suddenly DeLong, in a loud, commanding voice, barked, "This is the police. Heave to and prepare to be boarded." The words, amplified by the bullhorn, echoed dimly through the hull.

"Oh, what's happening?"

The engines changed pitch again, gaining speed, and the boat leaned. Susan clutched the steps to avoid being thrown off her feet. Voices, this time on the radio, but she only caught a word every now and again. Two pairs of legs left the bridge and went outside. She couldn't stand it. She hoisted herself up the steps and bounded past Harkey at the wheel then out onto the deck.

Danny had his back to her and leaned around the starboard side of the cutter looking toward the bow. Susan went to the port side. A few feet in front of her an RCMP officer crouched, one hand grasping the yellow, tube-like railing, the other clutching a gun!

When she peered intently into the fog ahead a strong wind stung her eyes. She blinked away the blurring. They must be chasing the fishing boat. Must be. But the thumping of the engines obliterated any other sounds and the fog settled around the coastal islands in a dense wall. But there! Up ahead, a shadowy outline.

Susan started when a brawny arm encircled her waist. "You should be below." Danny spoke into her ear but didn't pull her away from the corner.

"Are you sure that's them?"

"They're up to no good all right, look at 'em run."

She chanced a look at his face—eyebrows lowered, clenched teeth bared.

"They're headed into that mess of rocks!"

He rushed into the bridge. She slid along the wall and peeked inside. Danny and Harkey, voices garbled, looked back and forth from the radar to the porthole.

Danny screamed exuberantly, "Yes! Yes!" and swung a fist through the air.

What? Susan scrambled back around the side and pulled herself up onto the fore deck and peered over the Mountie's head. There, in the fog, two outlines—the bulky fishing boat and, converging upon it, a different boat. Long and low, it flew across the water, closing the distance by the second. She knew the dark wood hull and green cabins. Rummy!

Susan bellowed, "Go get him, Rummy!"

Rummy maneuvered in front of the kidnappers. Susan cringed, expecting to hear a crunch of collision. The fishing boat veered off and slowed.

The cutter, engines thrilled, water churning, decelerated a dozen yards from the kidnappers. Susan gasped in recognition; the raised partitions on the deck, the pointed swordfish stand on the prow! It was the boat that she and Amy had been taken on that terrifying night.

A man appeared on its deck. She saw the flash from the muzzle of a gun and ducked instinctively. The Mounties returned fire, two shots.

The noise was deafening. It reverberated inside her entire body, leaving her breathless. Terrified, she hid behind the bridge with her hands wrapped over her wailing ears.

Crack! Bing! A chip of yellow paint landed on her knee. The noise abruptly stopped. She considered going below; it was dangerous outside. But, what if Amy was on their deck. Was that why the shooting had stopped? She crawled to the corner and peered around.

The fishing boat was so close that she could see paint strokes where someone had painted a white scallop on the turquoise hull. She looked further aft and saw the same dark-haired man who had punched her the night on the beach. An oily curl of hair stuck to his forehead.

Susan leaped to her feet. He had Amy by the arm!

Amy didn't struggle at all when he lifted her high onto his chest to use as a human shield. Her tiny foot landed on the gunwale and a fluorescent-orange shoelace coiled toward the water.

Susan studied the child's dirty face and lank hair; darkness circled her eyes, her complexion was sallow, and her head lolled listlessly. Suddenly DeLong, obscuring her view for an instant, jumped from the superstructure and entered the bridge.

"Get them on the radio," he immediately commanded. "I'm not going to conduct this negotiation by screaming. Get them on the radio!"

Because the engines were idled, his words were clearly heard. He demanded to speak to the man holding Amy. The man, presumably in response to something said by someone inside the fishing boat, backed up toward the overhang section and dropped Amy to the deck.

DeLong yelled into the mike, "Speak your piece." After a pause, "Hand over the kid first. Why should we trust you?"

Amy peeked her head over the gunwale and looked glassy-eyed at the cutter. Susan plastered a brave smile on her face but Amy didn't respond so she waved her arms in big, wide arcs. Amy recognized her! Her eyes cleared and the indomitable spark Susan had often seen on the beach returned. She had a tremendous urge to fling herself over the side and swim to the kidnappers' boat.

"It's okay, sweetie," she called. "It won't be long now."

The child stared back with huge brown eyes. Suddenly she disappeared. After a couple of anxious seconds, she appeared further along where the gunwale wasn't so high. Susan was trying to think of something encouraging to call over when her heart jumped to her throat. Face in set determination, Amy leaned out. Her entire body rolled slowly over the wooden rail, arms flailed an instant, and then she splashed into the water and vanished. Susan screamed and leaned forward until suspended half over the water herself. It was ten feet from the water's surface to the top of the rail.

"Amy!" The waves lifted her into view, then dropped her out of sight. "Throw her a life preserver!"

No one appeared on the kidnapper's deck. They were too immersed in the negotiations with the police. Susan caught sight of one pale hand in the water. "Someone! Amy's overboard! Help her!"

Susan yanked off the slicker, heeled off her shoes, climbed to the top of the railing, teetered there a heartbeat, and then dove into the water. She swam with every fiber of her muscles. After a long minute, an enormous swell carried her yards from where Amy had gone under. Sputtering and gasping, she churned her feet and searched. No sign of the child. She ignored the sting of the salt on her eyes and put her face into the water to peer through the murkiness. There, a flash of fluorescence. She fought her way over and reached Amy before she went under again.

After grabbing the child's wrists, she wiggled around and pulled her arms over her head so that she rode on her back. Amy, hacking and coughing, squeezed tightly on Susan's neck.

Susan chanced another glance up at the boat. No one.

She kicked around to look back at the cutter. Three men were silhouetted against the fog, two RCMP on the bow, and Danny on the aft. She guessed that they'd seen her but were trying not to look at her, trying to avoid alerting the kidnappers.

She could swim back to the cutter, but then they'd be out in the open. What to do? Should she swim to the far side of the fishing boat where Rummy's boat idled? Susan vacillated in fear. What if the kidnappers revved up the engines? They'd be run over! Should she swim to the rear? No, the waters would be too turbulent and the rudder could knock them.

She struck off with powerful breaststrokes toward the bow. Amy hung on so tightly that it constricted Susan's breathing, but better that than to have her slide off. Surely everyone could hear her splashing and grunting?

As she rounded the bow, Susan saw Rummy's boat pointed toward her, a mere half-dozen yards away! With renewed determination she yanked her arms, pushing the water. If she could just get Amy safe it would make up for everything.

"Get back here or I'll shoot!"

Susan gasped and gulped salt water. Coughing, wheezing, she squeezed her eyes and swam with all her strength. Amy was on her back; she had to shelter her. Oh, no! Was that a bullet she heard? Yes, shooting! The solid hull of Rummy's boat loomed. Finally she struggled around to its lee side out of the line of fire. A thick hemp rope ladder tumbled over the side. Rummy exchanged a grin with her, and then shot a fearful glance behind him.

"Hold on! Stay put!" he hollered, then disappeared.

"Oh, Amy." She gasped. "Let go of my neck now. That's a girl. Hang on this rope. Good girl."

Rummy pulled them clear of the water. Landing on the deck, one arm holding Amy snugly against her body, the realization of what she'd done hit Susan. She knelt there, water streaming off her, and jammed her knuckles between her teeth to keep from sobbing.

* * *

An hour later, Danny ducked through the door and stepped softly into the inner cabin of the *Jacques II.* Neither Susan nor Amy heard him. One foot on a stool, Susan leaned forward and rolled up the cuff of one of Rummy's paint-stained overalls. A curtain of hair hid her face. Although her figure was obliterated by the soft, baggy cotton, she moved gracefully. As she dropped to her knees before Amy to fastened the top button of the bulky shirt the child wore, he cleared his throat.

Susan turned with a smile, rose, and took a step toward him. Apparently something in his expression made her hesitate. Amy scampered off the bench and hid behind her legs.

For the child's sake, Danny didn't want to make a scene, but he was so overcome with emotions that he wanted to gather Susan in his arms. She was safe now; they were both safe now. When the Mountie had reported that she had gone over the side he instantly abandoned the wheel and prepared to dive in after her.

DeLong had stopped him. "We already know she's a strong swimmer. And maybe they won't notice the kid's gone."

Danny never again wanted to suffer those moments of anguish—unable to take his eyes off her, yet not wanting to draw anyone else's attention to where she swam through the inky water.

Amy, dark eyes and tangled black hair, peeked around a leg. Her trust in Susan made him smile.

Danny dropped to her eye level saying, "Hello, you must be Amy. My name's Danny." She disappeared behind the baggy pants. He tried again. "The captain of this boat has your Mommy on the radio, ah, the telephone. Would you like to talk to her?"

She thrust her face forward, hopeful but not quite trusting, then yanked on Susan's arm and implored, "Can I?"

"Of course." Susan hoisted her on her hip and swung her through the door to the main cabin.

Rummy, hair askew, perched on a three-legged stool before the radio equipment. "Hold your horses now, Mrs. Sutherland, she's right here."

Susan deposited Amy on the second stool and helped Rummy settle the bulky, cushioned earphones in place. Suddenly Amy's eyes expanded and her mouth formed a round circle.

"Speak into this, honey," Susan said hoarsely and angled the microphone.

Amy squealed, "Mommy! Hi, Mommy! Yes, I love you too, Mommy. Can I come home now?"

The moment Susan turned her tear-brimmed eyes toward him, Danny opened his arms and folded her close.

"Hey, hey, you did well," he whispered, patting her back.

Her bottom lip trembled. "I was so scared."

"Aw, Sus," Danny said.

Rummy's gruff voice interrupted. "Being as there's a couple of mighty anxious parents waiting back in Seal Harbor, do ya think you can hold off on the mushy stuff a while?"

Danny dragged his eyes away from Susan's. "The Sutherlands? They're already in Seal Harbor?"

"Yep," Rummy said. "According to that RCMP fellow, didn't have much choice after Susan got things stirred up. Told the cops everything. He and the missus were trying to do what the kidnappers wanted. Didn't have much choice, I guess."

Susan sighed. "Oh, what a horrible week this must have been for them. No wonder Deidra acted that way to me. She must have been terrified I'd do something to . . ." She swallowed her words and glanced toward Amy who, in the irrepressibility of youth, babbled to her mother while she twisted and turned the dials on the radio.

Rummy rushed to rescue his set. He patted Amy's chubby fingers and shook his head sternly. She grinned impishly and patted his fingers right back.